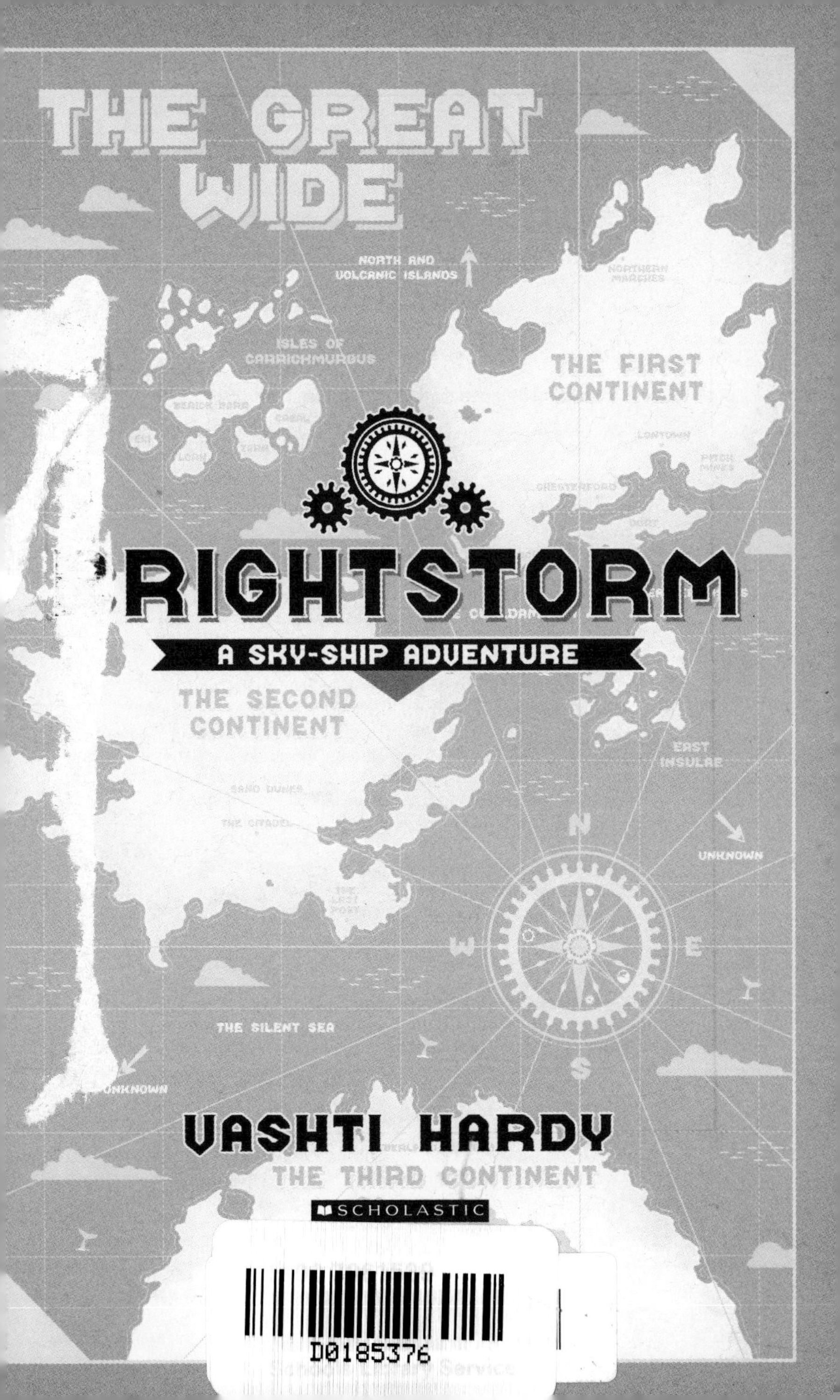

THE GREAT WIDE
NORTH AND VOLCANIC ISLANDS
NORTHERN MARCHES
ISLES OF CARRICHMURGUS
THE FIRST CONTINENT
LONTOWN
PITCH MINES
CHESTERFORD
RIGHTSTORM
A SKY-SHIP ADVENTURE
THE SECOND CONTINENT
EAST INSULAE
SAND DUNES
THE CITADEL
N
UNKNOWN
W
E
THE SILENT SEA
S
UNKNOWN
VASHTI HARDY
THE THIRD CONTINENT
SCHOLASTIC
D0185376

Scholastic Children's Books
An imprint of Scholastic Ltd
Euston House, 24 Eversholt Street, London, NW1 1DB, UK
Registered office: Westfield Road, Southam, Warwickshire, CV47 0RA
SCHOLASTIC and associated logos are trademarks and/or registered
trademarks of Scholastic Inc.

First published in the UK by Scholastic Ltd, 2018

Text copyright © Vashti Hardy, 2018

The right of Vashti Hardy to be identified as the
author of this work has been asserted by her.

ISBN 978 1407 18170 7

A CIP catalogue record for this book
is available from the British Library.

All rights reserved.
This book is sold subject to the condition that it shall not, by
way of trade or otherwise, be lent, hired out or otherwise circulated
in any form of binding or cover other than that in which it is published.
No part of this publication may be reproduced, stored in a retrieval
system, or transmitted in any form or by any means (electronic,
mechanical, photocopying, recording or otherwise) without
prior written permission of Scholastic Limited.

Printed by CPI Group (UK) Ltd, Croydon, CR0 4YY
Papers used by Scholastic Children's Books are made
from wood grown in sustainable forests.

7 9 10 8 6

This is a work of fiction. Names, characters, places, incidents
and dialogues are products of the author's imagination or are used
fictitiously. Any resemblance to actual people, living or dead,
events or locales is entirely coincidental.

www.scholastic.co.uk

For Meg, Sammy, Poppy and Darren,
my crew.

WITHDRAWN

HAMPSHIRE
COUNTY LIBRARY
H 00 7061539
Peters 28-Feb-2019
£6.99
9781407181707

CHAPTER 1

BRIGHTSTORM

The heavy chug of a sky-ship firing its engines rumbled through Lontown.

"Quick, pull me up!" Arthur called from the lower roof.

"Clamp your hand on to the pipe – see if it's strong enough to take your weight," said Maudie.

"We're going to miss it, Maud!"

"We're not, it's only just fired up, and if you hadn't been so engrossed in *Volcanic Islands of the North*..."

"If you hadn't insisted on adjusting my arm..."

"So, we both lost track of the chime. Come on,

Arty, I want to see if the modification to the fingers helped."

Arthur sighed. Using his left hand he raised the iron arm attached to his right shoulder, then folded the metal fingers around the pipe. But as he tried to pull himself up, it juddered and slipped down.

Maudie shook her head and looked away in thought. "They need more tension."

"Just help me up, will you?"

"Perhaps if I use Harris screws," she said.

Arthur found a small jut of brick about halfway up the wall between upper and lower roof, and used it to launch himself with his left foot. He narrowly grabbed the lip of the roof and swung his other leg so that his foot hooked the edge, then he heaved his body up. "Thanks for nothing, Maud."

"You totally had it, Arty."

Their eyes met. "Race you to the top!" they said together, then scrambled up the tiles like a pair of wild cats.

They reached the topmost part of the roof at the same time and straddled the ridge, out of breath and laughing.

"Poacher will freak if she catches us up here again," Maudie said.

"It won't be the first time."

"Or the last."

At that moment, the sky-ship rose from the distant docks above the domes and spires of the city skyline. Maudie took her uniscope from her tool belt. "Standard double engine... Ooh, dipped haltway fans and a swivel blade propeller – good choice."

"Let me see!" Arthur said, tugging the uniscope from her hands. "I bet Jemima Jones is at the helm. I read that her father was letting her captain the first flight."

"Look at the balloon shape. Is that two montgolfieres?" Maudie snatched the uniscope back.

"And have they positioned the sail in between?"

"Yes, you're right."

"Strange..."

"... Choice. And it's smaller than I expected for a new sky-ship."

"Well, they only need to get to Creal. The Joneses don't care about the far reaches of the Wide; they only care about exploring caves to find gems."

"Or maybe they're just looking for a shortcut. They say the caves of Creal are so deep that they reach all the way to Tarn."

They fell silent as the sky-ship flew towards them, over the great dome of the Geographical Society, as was tradition for the start of every expedition, before turning west and chugging into the distance.

Arthur glanced across at Maudie. The red ribbon holding back a lock of rusty brown hair had come loose and dangled across her forehead. Her freckles blushed bright in the sunlight and her eyes were set in a concentrated frown. Every feature of Maudie's face mirrored Arthur's almost perfectly, and he knew her thoughts at that moment were exactly the same as his.

He squeezed her shoulder. "He'll be back soon."

"It might be another moon-cycle, or more if they've hit bad weather."

"I hope not. I'm not sure I can put up with Poacher for that long!"

Maudie pulled the ribbon from her hair and gave it to Arthur. He passed it under a strand of her hair and pulled it to the side. Maudie took the other end and between them they made a bow. They had always tied it together from a young age. Dad said it would be a good way to help Arthur learn to be twice as skilled with one hand.

Something caught his eye below – a woman walked briskly across the square. "Who's that?"

"I don't know, but she seems to be heading towards our house."

"Then let's see if we can get there before Poacher!"

They skittered down the tiles and on to the flat section of roof outside Arthur's room. As Arthur scrambled through the open window, two steely knocks echoed through Brightstorm House.

The footsteps of Mistress Poacher clonked along the corridor below. For someone so thin she made quite an impact.

They barged out of his room, down the stairway, and past the housekeeper, sending her into a full spin as they raced along the hallway.

"Well, really! I should hope it's your father back to teach you some manners."

Arthur could imagine her narrow-eyed glare behind them, her lips squeezed tight as though tasting something sour.

Maudie reached the door first and flung it

wide. There was a dumpy woman with grey curly hair melding into the great furry collar of her coat. She frowned and looked between them. "Is your guardian here?"

"We don't have one," Arthur said.

"Or need one," Maudie added, glancing over her shoulder at Mistress Poacher.

"We have a father. . ."

"But he's on an expedition."

The woman pushed her spectacles up the bridge of her nose. Her gaze rested for a moment on where Arthur's right arm would have been, if he'd had one.

"A snake attacked him in the Northern Marshes. Arthur killed him with a knife."

The woman's frown deepened. "How shocking."

Arthur shrugged. "I didn't have a choice; it was me or the snake."

The furry collar of her jacket moved. Arthur blinked and looked at Maudie to see if she'd seen it too.

Mistress Poacher put her arms between the twins and prised them apart. "This is the Brightstorm residence. Can I help you?"

"Are you in charge?"

Mistress Poacher lifted her chin. "Yes."

"My name is Madame Gainsford."

It was vaguely familiar, but Arthur couldn't quite place it.

Madame Gainsford blinked several times and pursed her lips as though the whole business of standing on the doorstep made her feel unwell. "May I come inside and talk with you?" Her eyes briefly flicked down to the twins. "Alone?"

The fur collar moved again. This time it raised a head and winked. It wasn't a fur collar at all – she had an animal draped around her neck! Then Arthur remembered where he'd heard the name; Madame Gainsford was on the Council of the Lontown Geographical Society. "Is it about Dad?" he blurted out.

"Are they nearly home?" Maudie added.

But their questions hung unanswered as Mistress Poacher pushed them out of the way and ushered Madame Gainsford along the hallway to the library. They followed behind, but Mistress Poacher put a firm hand up.

"You two can get back to..." she waved her hand, "whatever it is you spend your days doing." She turned to Madame Gainsford. "Any sensible father would have sent them to boarding school for a proper education, but I suppose new explorer families don't hold the same values as the genuine bloodlines."

Then, with a dull thud, the door shut.

"Did you hear that? Genuine bloodline, what nonsense," Arthur said.

"More to the point, did you see that thing?" Maudie said.

"Around her neck!"

"I know!"

"It actually moved."

"I think it was a stoat."

"And definitely a sapient."

There was the scrape of chairs being pulled out. Maudie put a finger to her lips, but no matter how closely they pressed their ears to the door, all they could hear was hushed talk.

"I wish we *had* been to the Northern Marshes," Arthur whispered.

"We will one day." Maudie smiled. She began drumming her fingers silently on the wall. "Maybe he's been delayed. It's probably a problem with the sky-ship – I told him he needed a better flexer pump. He's likely stuck in the Second Continent somewhere, unable to find replacement parts."

Arthur nodded, but a strange fear rose inside him.

The door suddenly opened. Madame Gainsford hurried past without looking at either of them. The stoat scurried at her heels and jumped back up around her neck as she let herself out the front door.

"That didn't take long," Maudie whispered.

The fire had gone out in the library hearth and Mistress Poacher sat at the dark oak table, her hands clasped so tightly that the veins in her wrist stuck out. Mistress Poacher was a late replacement housekeeper hired just before Dad had left for the expedition, and they'd soon discovered the smiles of her initial interview were just a show she'd put on for Dad. Every sound they made seemed to irritate her – she, like many in Lontown, thought children should be invisible. Not like Dad, who always had time for them.

Her shoulders rose as she took a breath, and her gaze flickered between them. Arthur was sure her usual harshness had softened, and there was a rare glimpse of warmth, or was it a glimmer of pity? But she straightened up, and it disappeared.

"Your father's not coming back."

Her statement seemed to hang in the air without meaning.

Arthur and Maudie exchanged a glance.

"What did you say?" Maudie asked.

Mistress Poacher raised her eyebrows. "He's not coming back, so you'd better find a way to get used to it."

Arthur felt as though a great hole was opening beneath his feet, pulling him inside. "What do you mean?"

"He's perished in the Third Continent – that's all I know."

Her words were lead.

She stood up and brushed her hands on her pinafore as though ridding herself of what she'd just said. She walked stiffly to the door. The crinkle of her long black skirt stopped as she paused outside. "I always said you were too indulged, living in books about far-off lands, and messing about all day with tools. Now you'll have to face the real world." She sighed. "There's a hearing in the morning at nine chimes at the Geographical Society. We'll find out more then."

And then she left them.

That night they took the blankets from Dad's bed and curled up amongst the books and tools in the library. Dad's chair remained beside the fireplace, exactly where he'd left it. If they both thought really hard, they could imagine he was sitting there, his head resting in the indentation on the cushion, his sun-blushed, freckled face smiling down at them, and his large hands placed on the frayed arms, fingers picking at the loose threads as he told them a story about his early adventures.

Not a word passed between them for a long time. Arthur had always missed Dad terribly when he went away, but now he knew he was never coming back, it felt as though his heart had split inside him, and a great door had slammed on a future that had been so certain before – the trips the three of them were going to make, all the places in the Wide they would discover together, how he was going to teach them how to navigate and fly the *Violetta*.

"I miss him so much," Maudie whispered.

And all Arthur could do was swallow back the tears.

CHAPTER 2

BAD TO WORSE

In the morning, Mistress Poacher escorted them through the streets of Uptown towards the great dome of the Geographical Society.

The siblings were silent as they trudged along, still trying to make sense of the terrible news. Arthur's iron arm jostled against his side, banging out a numbing rhythm with every other step. Maudie had etched a Brightstorm moth on to a flat metal panel just above the wrist, and it now reflected a dancing patch of light on to walls along the street as they walked.

As the watchtower began its first chime of nine,

they turned the corner to the Lontown Geographical Society. The square bustled with people filtering towards the Society building. A few people stared as they noticed Arthur's iron arm. He tried not to feel self-conscious – people stared if he wore it, they stared more if he didn't. Dad had always told him not to care what people thought, but it seemed harder without his father by his side.

Arthur paused to watch a group buzzing around a nearby *Lontown Chronicle* stand. He caught a glimpse of the headline. *BREAKING – Death in the Frozen South – What Really Happened? Speculation Rises.* Arthur tried to swallow, but his throat tightened. Maudie was staring too.

Mistress Poacher glanced over her shoulder. "Come along." Then she paused, and for a moment Arthur thought she would say something kind. Instead she took a comb from her bag and passed it to him. "For goodness' sake, run this through your hair, Arthur. Your father may have found it acceptable for you to run wild, but you can't very well be in the company of the finest in Lontown with hair worse than a floor brush. Maudie, you should be wearing the skirt I laid out for you, not those old house slacks. At least tuck in your shirts, both of you." She tutted.

They followed her up the stone steps, through the carved doorway, and into a grand hall. Majestic pillars and gilt-framed maps lined the walls, illuminated by glittering chandeliers. Statues of the great explorers with notable achievements stared from the sides. All around, the hall bustled with the people of Lontown, chatter and anticipation fizzing in the air. The sound made Arthur want to scream out; how could anything carry on as normal when his world had been ripped apart? He forced himself to focus – he had to get through this, for Maudie, if not himself. She looked across and he knew she was thinking the same for him.

They pushed onwards towards the double doors of the auditorium. Some of the most respected explorer families in Lontown walked ahead of them – Rumpole Blarthington, five times as wide as his wife beside him, dressed in a plush velvet coat and top hat. Dad said he'd never achieved much and lived a lavish life on the exploration achievements of his great grandmother. Arthur glimpsed Evelyn Acquafreeda to his side: a tiny woman in iridescent blue jacket and trousers, as though it had been made from the skin of an exotic sea creature. She upheld her family tradition of refusing to embrace the advances from sea- to sky-ships, and preferred to persist solely with ocean exploration. Hilda Hilbury pushed past Maudie, her nose in the air. "Do excuse me," she said, sounding as though she didn't much care to be excused at all. She stood half a head taller than most in the room, even without her ribboned flowerpot hat, her stature matching her family's achievements in claiming the peaks of most of the mountains in the First Continent.

In the auditorium, people were bustling around filling seats, so Mistress Poacher hurried Arthur and Maudie to a few vacant chairs on their right. Soon, a loud clang rang through the room as the great doors behind them shut, to disappointed shouts on the other side.

A great arc of people gathered on the stage at the front. Arthur tried to make out who they were. Most seemed to be officials from the Geographical Society, and another group dressed in a less exuberant, more severe style. Madame Gainsford banged a hammer on the table and, after a few last scuffles, silence fell. One woman transfixed Arthur. Her beauty was undeniable. She was dressed from head to toe in a pale shade of pink, and on her jacket she wore a distinctive silver brooch in the shape of an exotic insect, something like the dragonflies of the Northern Marshes but larger, perhaps something replicating a creature from the tropical east. He'd seen her picture in the *Lontown Chronicle* – Eudora Vane, of the most famous explorer family in Lontown. She was the leader of the other expedition that had been trying to reach South Polaris alongside his father's.

Madame Gainsford stood up. "Esteemed members of the Geographical Society and the many . . . interested citizens of Lontown, this urgent meeting has been called to determine the truth of recent events. The expedition to South Polaris was intended to uncover what lies at the southernmost point on the compass, expanding our knowledge of geography and the very structure of this planet. As reported, the expedition not only failed in its main objective, but ended in catastrophe."

Whispered chatter rippled around the auditorium. Arthur and Maudie drew closer together.

"Madame Vane, perhaps if you would address the board first. Can you tell us exactly what happened?"

Eudora Vane stood up. Her voice carried through the hall, clear and honeyed. "We were in the Second Continent at the Last Post. We landed our sky-ship, the *Victorious*, for the night to replenish a few last supplies and for the crew to rest before heading off again at first light. Pitch supplies were scarce, but we'd managed to stock up with just enough to make it across to the Third Continent and back."

Maudie leant in towards Arthur and whispered, "Please let him not have been foolish enough to run out of pitch in the Third Continent."

Arthur didn't answer. Dad was meticulous at calculating fuel.

"The Brightstorm sky-ship, the *Violetta*, landed at the Last Post shortly afterwards. We exchanged greetings and ate together around a fire in the spirit of comrade explorers, even though, of course, we were rivals to reach South Polaris first. We wished each other luck and went to bed, each needing to take the opportunity of gathering strength before the perilous journey ahead. Little did we know it was the last time we'd see them alive."

The auditorium hung off her every word. There was complete silence. Arthur tried to steady his breathing as a great black wave of sadness washed over him, pressing down, drowning him. He looked around the auditorium, searching in the vain hope that Dad would appear, that it was all a terrible mistake.

"During the night, I was woken by the hum of the *Violetta*'s engines. At first I thought they were trying to get an advantage. I wasn't concerned, as I knew the *Victorious* was the faster ship and would catch up." Madame Vane paused, a frown bending her brow. "Perhaps my chief engineer, Mr Wicketts, should take it from here."

A man further along the line stood up, the screech of his chair rasping through the theatre. He was obviously much less comfortable speaking to such a huge crowd. He coughed. Then mumbled something.

"You'll need to speak up, Mr Wicketts," Madame Gainsford said, shaking her head.

Mr Wicketts cleared his throat. "The engines of

the *Violetta* woke me too. I thought I'd better make a start on the engine checks, as Madame Vane would be sure to want to take off soon. I went down to the engine room and the stores. I couldn't believe what I saw." He paused.

"What did you see, Mr Wicketts?"

He turned his palms upward. "It was almost empty."

The audience gasped.

Madame Gainsford frowned deeply. "Mr Wicketts, could you elaborate for us?"

He cleared his throat. "The outside hatch had been broken. A great hole gaped in the bottom of the *Victorious* so I could see the ground below. The pitch had been stolen, and the *Violetta* had already taken off. The only other person at the Last Post was the watcher, and she could hardly empty a ship of pitch alone in the night. I mean, the population is hardly booming down there. Besides, we questioned her, but she had an alibi. She'd been invited up to the ship's mess for a drink with Captain Vane and the rest of the crew."

Madame Gainsford narrowed her gaze. "Just to be absolutely clear, Mr Wicketts, are you suggesting that your supplies were stolen by the Brightstorm crew?"

He nodded.

The audience erupted as people turned to those nearby to exclaim their thoughts.

Maudie grabbed Arthur's hand.

"Dad wouldn't do that," Arthur said, his voice shaking.

Madame Vane raised her hand a little and the audience quieted to listen. "Perhaps I should continue."

A couple in front of Arthur and Maudie began looking over their shoulders at them. They tapped the people in front and said something. Soon a ripple of whispers fluttered through the audience with more people turning to look. Maudie squeezed his left hand tighter and Arthur did his best to ignore the stares and focus on Madame Vane.

"We weren't going to give up on our dream of reaching South Polaris that easily, so we used the little fuel that remained in our stores to head back inland to find more pitch. It cost us valuable days and we paid a hefty price. Then we battled onwards across the sea, where the rough weather was every bit as terrible as reported, and set us back again.

"On reaching the Third Continent, we crossed a great frozen forest. Beyond were enormous sheer mountains, too high for a sky-ship's balloons. We were forced to land on a snow plain before an expansive icy lake which skirted the mountains as far as could be seen. Our calculations told us that South Polaris was on the other side of the mountains. The only way forward was on foot.

"We saw the Brightstorm ship had landed nearby. We assumed an advance party had proceeded and left the rest of the crew at the ship, but when we approached the *Violetta*, we found it was completely empty. Everything was left as though the whole crew had suddenly abandoned it. There were tools discarded, equipment strewn. The fuel tanks were nearly full, at a far higher level than they should have been. But the crew had simply disappeared."

"Disappeared?"

"Yes. As we looked more closely it was apparent from the state of disarray there'd been a terrible fight. Then we saw them."

"The crew?"

Eudora Vane shook her head and looked at the

floor. She'd become pale. "Despite what they had done to us, I wouldn't wish this upon any fellow explorers."

"Go on."

"We found traces of animal tracks around their ship, but like nothing we have come across before in all our travels of the Wide. There were huge paw prints, the length of two human feet at least. The Brightstorm crew had clearly been attacked by wild beasts. There were traces of blood in the snow but nothing else. I fear not one had survived."

Arthur's breath caught in his lungs. It was too horrible to take in.

"Madame Vane, did you see these foul creatures?"

"Yes." She signalled to someone at the side of the auditorium. "The crew managed to capture one." The audience gasped audibly, and two of her men disappeared backstage for a moment, then returned carrying what appeared to be an enormous pile of fur between them. Leaning forward, Arthur saw two pointed shapes – ears, a great black nose and teeth like daggers. It was an animal pelt. They threw it down on the table before the members of the Geographical Society as the audience began muttering in horrified astonishment.

Madame Gainsford walked around the pelt inspecting it. "This creature's shoulders must have reached the height of a human."

"Indeed," said Madame Vane.

The stoat buried its head in Madame Gainsford's collar.

"Do continue with your recount, Madame Vane."

"We still wanted to try and reach beyond the mountains to South Polaris, to salvage something from the disaster, but we soon realized the lake had become impassable; a sudden thaw had set in and the ice was terribly unstable. We couldn't be sure of getting across safely, let alone back. The mountains stretched as wide as we could see and the lake was too vast. We didn't have enough equipment to go onwards and morale was low after what we'd been through."

The board nodded, agreeing with her decision.

"We travelled back, knowing we'd need to make another attempt when the weather was favourable and we were better equipped for the mountain crossing." Eudora Vane dipped her head and sat down.

Madame Gainsford shuffled the papers before her, then stood up. "Thank you, Madame Vane. If that is all your crew has to say on the matter?" She paused, but the crew remained silent. "The board will discuss and reach a conclusion tomorrow." She turned to the audience. "Since neither expedition managed to reach South Polaris after all, we will also discuss the possibility of relaunching the prize fund. As no one has encountered this impenetrable ring of mountains before, it is clear further exploration is needed to find a way through. I would like a full report of what you observed, Madame Vane."

Close by, Arthur heard a man mutter that Ernest Brightstorm and his crew got what they'd deserved if they'd broken the code, that it was nature's way of justice. The woman beside him said that it was proof there was no place for new-blood explorers; they didn't respect the old ways and should leave it to the respected families.

The people looking at them weren't the kindly eyes of people concerned that two children had just lost their only parent. They were all looking at them as though they were seeing Ernest Brightstorm, and they'd already judged him.

CHAPTER 3

CLAUSE ONE HUNDRED AND FIFTY-TWO

That afternoon, time in the library stood still. If Arthur thought hard enough he could imagine the past two days had never happened and Dad had just nipped to the larder for honey to spread on sweet bread. Mistress Poacher had escorted them back to the house, then had disappeared again, saying she had things to take care of.

Arthur picked a book from the shelf, *Exploring in the Third Age*, and Maudie sat down in front of his iron arm. "I'm going to adjust the fingers, and it needs a polish. You've been neglecting it," she said quietly.

They sat in silence, Arthur not reading the words before him, and Maudie buffing his iron arm until it shone like sun on a still pool.

After a while Arthur looked across. "Maud, we've still got each other, we've still got home. Dad had insurance; he will have made sure we're all right."

But nothing seemed to be all right.

Later, the front door banged and clonky footsteps could be heard along the hallway coming towards them. Maudie frowned at Arthur.

Mistress Poacher opened the library door. A man stood beside her in a crisp suit buttoned tightly at the waist, long tails, and a shirt with cuffs that Dad would have called unnecessarily flouncy. They matched the handkerchief in his pocket and the frill of his brooch-pinned necktie. He walked forward without moving his upper body, making him appear as though he was floating along. Regarding them with stone serious eyes, he tipped his hat.

Arthur and Maudie looked at each other.

The man enclosed Arthur's left hand with his own hands and shook it. His hands were cold and sent shivers the length of Arthur's back.

"Bartemaus Smethwyck," he said, the muscles in his face remaining rigid as he spoke.

The chill feeling stuck to Arthur's hand.

"Take a seat, Mr Smethwyck. I'll fetch some tea," said Mistress Poacher.

The man moved to take a chair at the table, then looked across at Ernest Brightstorm's chair and sat there.

Maudie's lips were so tight, Arthur thought she would pop.

The twins stood before the guest as he placed his briefcase on his lap, took some papers from within, then folded his hands on top. Not waiting for Mistress Poacher's return, he said, "I represent the underwriters of the insurance policy your father took out for the Brightstorm expedition to South Polaris. The life insurance policy your father purchased set out that you were to receive the house, contents and a lump sum, and I believe he instructed his solicitor that in the event of misfortune, Mistress Poacher was to stay on and take care of you until you reached sixteen."

Arthur let out a breath. He could handle Mistress Poacher, as long as they were at Brightstorm House.

"Except," Mr Smethwyck paused. "There is clause one hundred and fifty-two."

Arthur and Maudie exchanged a look as the insurance representative ran his finger down the pages until he reached the relevant section.

Mr Smethwyck gave a small cough. "*If* the Explorer's Code, as laid out by Lontown Geographical Society, has been broken, all insurance is invalidated and we have the right to seize all assets with immediate effect."

"But nothing's been decided!" Maudie said.

"The board agreed, with a majority vote this morning, that the Brightstorm expedition were guilty of stealing fuel from the *Victorious*, and so had indeed broken the Explorer's Code."

Arthur's blood drained to his feet. "But this can't be right! We need to speak to our father's solicitor."

"There is nothing anyone can do. This is your father's signature on the insurance document in black and white."

"But he knew he would never break the code, so he wouldn't have cared about this clause one hundred and whatever!" Arthur said.

"Clearly that isn't the case."

At that moment, they heard a brash knock on the front door.

"I'm sure Mistress Poacher will see to that," Mr Smethwyck said.

Shortly, more footsteps trailed along the corridor. A troop of people burst into the room carrying great crates.

The strangers began rifling through the contents of the library, bundling books into the crates and taking the pictures off the walls and the ornaments from the shelves.

"You can't do this!" Arthur said.

"I'm afraid we can," Mr Smethwyck said.

"Don't touch that!" Maudie said, hugging her tool belt to her chest. "This was my mother's; you have no right!"

Arthur felt frozen. He was jolted into action when a man packing a crate full of books reached for *Volcanic Islands of the North*, which lay on the table. They tussled, but Arthur lost his grip on the book and a single page ripped away in his hand. The man glared and put the book into his crate.

Then another picked up Arthur's iron arm and

said something to his colleague about it making a good sovereign if it was melted down.

"Don't you dare," Maudie said, grabbing it. She looked as though she would clobber the next person attempting to take it. "This belongs to my brother."

Watching Dad's possessions being rifled through and thrown into boxes was awful. "We'll find a way to get everything back; we've still got a home," Arthur whispered to Maudie.

But Mr Smethwyck was suddenly beside him. "I'm afraid that 'seizing all assets' includes the house. This is no longer Brightstorm property."

"But we've lived here our whole lives. Where will we go?" Maudie cried.

"I believe that Mistress Poacher remains your guardian; you will go with her."

All they could do was watch, utterly helpless as their life was dismantled around them. When everyone and everything had gone, they sat alone on the bare floorboards. Arthur's whole body was numb. He looked at the page still clutched in his hand. It was the title page, featuring a captioned, full-colour illustration of the Brightstorm moth, discovered on one of the volcanic islands by Dad:

Ernest Brightstorm, the first ever Brightstorm explorer. It was a giant moth of brilliant fiery golds and reds with great feathery antennae, living against the odds in the hostile conditions of the volcanoes. Arthur folded the page, flipped open the top compartment of his iron arm and put it inside.

Mistress Poacher flung the door open. "Come along, I haven't got all day."

"Where will we live?" Maudie asked.

"We? Goodness, I know what it says on paper, but I can't possibly take care of you!"

As unhappy as Arthur felt about the prospect of Mistress Poacher looking after them for the foreseeable future, she was at least one familiar thing left that they could cling on to. "But Mr Smethwyck said you're our guardian now."

"I've packed you a bag each and made arrangements."

They followed her to the door.

Outside, a black cart waited. It was harnessed to a horse, not like the newer carriages of Uptown where pitch could drive a small engine. A couple perched on the front were dressed in black, tattered clothes, making them look like a pair of great crows.

Mistress Poacher shuffled Arthur and Maudie out of the door. "Luckily for you, I've found two people willing to take you on at short notice."

"Well now, Poacher, you never said one of them was. . ." The woman's eyes flitted to Arthur's iron arm which he held in his left. She turned to the man beside her. "Mr Beggins, I don't know if we can take this unsightly thing – he'll put me off my breakfast."

Mr Beggins squinted his already beady eyes and sniffed through his long nose. It wasn't a nice, distinctive nose that suited his face; it served to make him look spiteful. "They can eat in their room, Mrs Beggins. The shipyards are looking for cheap labour to mend the freight sky-ships, if the girl is as good with tools as Poacher says."

"But what'll the boy do in the shipyards with one arm?" She turned back to Mistress Poacher. "We'll just take the girl."

Maudie hooked Arthur's arm. "He's as capable as me."

Mistress Poacher hurried them towards the cart. "I can vouch for that. He's found a way around most problems, though he spends too much time with his head in books, dreaming. A dose of real Lontown will soon put paid to that."

Mrs Beggins stared. "We ain't Mr and Mrs Beggins' Home for the Unwanted Scraps of Lontown, you know."

"We're not unwanted. Our father loved us," Arthur said.

The woman sniffed. "From what I've heard, he was no better than the thieves of the Slumps. He was just a nobody reaching above his station."

"I'm not going anywhere without my brother!" Maudie's eyes were fierce but filming over. Arthur tried to swallow back his own rising emotion.

There was a pause. Then the man said, "Well, he might be useful around the house clearing up, don't you think, Mrs Beggins? Ain't you always saying Beggins Hall is too much for you? One can earn and one can cook and clean – it'll be like having our own servant."

Mrs Beggins' eyes lit up. "We'll be just like these Uptowners!"

Before they could even take in what was happening, Mistress Poacher bundled them into the cart.

"Let's be going to your new home," said Mr Beggins.

Arthur sat beside Maudie feeling as though a great unstoppable black wave was carrying them, and there was nothing they could do to stop it.

Out of the corner of his eye, Arthur saw Mrs Beggins pass a small pouch to Mistress Poacher. He heard the jangle of sovereigns. He jumped up. "You sold us!"

Mistress Poacher lifted her chin. "A small compensation for lost employment."

At that, Mr Beggins cracked his whip and Arthur was thrown back in his seat.

"Where are we going?" Maudie cried.

Mrs Beggins turned and gave a toothy smile that didn't have an inch of kindness in it. "To the Slumps, that's where."

Arthur and Maudie stared at each other. The Slumps was the poorest district of Lontown. It was rumoured that children were always disappearing from there, sent as slaves to work in the pitch mines to the south. Turning back to look at Brightstorm House, Arthur felt a piece of himself turn to stone inside.

They rode through increasingly narrow streets, everything becoming darker by the moment, until they were absorbed into the strange grey world of the Slumps of Lontown, where everything was covered in a layer of soot.

Beggins Hall was on a street of uneven cobblestones. The cart made their bones rattle inside as they clattered along. The house was tall and thin, as though the buildings either side were compressing it, and it was the grimiest of them all, with smoked out windows and dripping pipes.

"Right, Mr Beggins, you'd better get that horse back before old Cleghorn notices we took it, and I'll think about dinner."

Arthur realized how terribly hungry he felt, and the idea of a warm meal was at least something cheerful. They followed Mrs Beggins inside. Beggins Hall was as gloomy on the inside as out, with tattered curtains and ripped wallpaper hanging off the walls. The hallway had bare floorboards and felt colder than outside.

"I'll show you to your room."

The twins followed her up the three flights of narrow crooked stairs to a tiny door at the top of the house. Mrs Beggins opened the door and a chill draught escaped. Glimpses of grey sky could be seen through several holes in the roof. There were two mattresses and one dirty window.

"Here we are. I don't want to hear a peep out of you two – we maintain a calm, peaceful home."

Shouting and cursing ensued on the street outside. A baby was screaming in a house nearby.

"What chime is dinner, Mrs Beggins?" Maudie asked.

"Best you get making it soon. Mr Beggins isn't his kinder self when he's hungry."

"Us?"

"Of course – you need to earn your keep! There's a scraggleneck for stewing, which old Ratchett had going spare." She shut the door.

"Well, a scraggleneck sounds yummy," Arthur said.

Maudie looked at him. "And we didn't think things could get any worse."

CHAPTER 4

PARTHENA

Three moon-cycles passed in a numb routine of labour and sleep. Maudie was quickly set to work in the shipyards, while Arthur had the impossible task of keeping Beggins Hall clean, fetching supplies and cooking dinner. Moreover, Mrs Beggins was still taking offence to Arthur's lack of a right arm and made him wear his iron arm at all times. He loved his iron arm and how it could help him, but he wanted it to be his choice when he wore it. The shoulder strap rubbed if he wore it all the time and it became uncomfortable day in, day out. But the worst thing of all to Arthur: there wasn't a book in the house. Not one. The only thing to read was the *Lontown Chronicle*, and he could only sneak that away at the end of the day when the Begginses were snoring. It felt as though they'd been thrown into a terrible dream.

They didn't see a sovereign for their toils – Maudie must have earned back twice the amount the Begginses had paid Mistress Poacher. The siblings talked about running away, but even their rickety room was better than sleeping on the streets of the Slumps.

Every day, when Arthur had cooked dinner, he and Maudie would both serve it and stand at the edge of the shabby dining room, which Arthur called the Black Room on account of everything being black from floor to ceiling, even the table and two chairs. They stood watching the Begginses slobber and slurp the food down, waiting for the next command.

"I heard they've relaunched that challenge to reach South Polaris," Mrs Beggins said.

Arthur's heart missed a beat. He glanced at Maudie.

"Why anyone would want to leave Lontown

is beyond me," Mr Beggins said as he bit into a chicken leg, grease dripping down his hand.

"Who'd want to leave all this comfort?" Arthur mumbled under his breath to Maudie.

"Keep your mouth shut and one of you fetch the loaf," Mr Beggins said.

Mrs Beggins let out one of her silly high-pitched laughs. "I'll tell you why, Mr Beggins. One million sovereigns!"

"Not everyone does it for sovereigns," Maudie said, banging the loaf of bread on the table in front of Mrs Beggins.

"Watch what you're doing. That costs, you know!"

Maudie turned and walked back to join Arthur. "Sovereigns we earned," she muttered to him.

Mr Beggins threw down his chicken bone. "You cheeky blighter, I heard that. We give you a roof over your head, the kindness of our loving hearts. You're lucky you ain't scrabbling around on the streets."

"Now, Mr Beggins, don't you go upsetting yourself over these ungrateful wretches." Mrs Beggins pointed a pudgy finger at them. "There'll be no supper for either of you this evening."

Arthur's stomach rumbled. Mrs Beggins glared at him. "Now get out of my sight."

Maudie's cheeks flushed angry red and she took a step, but Arthur tugged her arm back. "Let's just go to our room."

"And there'll be no breakfast for you, either!" Mr Beggins called after them.

That evening, Arthur turned and fidgeted in his bed and tried to ignore his complaining stomach. He stared through the gaps in the roof at the stars, listening to the creak of the wooden beams. A cold draught licked over him and the scratch of small feet came from under the floorboards. He drew his legs up and felt the hairs on his body stand up. He hated rats, and Beggins Hall had dozens of them. Whenever he heard one he imagined it crawling all over him with its sharp little claws, long, worm-like tail and nibbling teeth.

He flung off his cover and climbed out of the window on to the rooftop. Silver-edged clouds drifted beyond the layered shapes of crooked roofs, bent chimneys, and washing lines. He balanced along the lip, then jumped the short distance to a ledge on the old ship watchtower next door. It was perhaps the one good thing about living at Beggins Hall.

"Hey, wait for me," Maudie called, lurching out of the window.

"Shh! You'll wake them."

"They're snoring away like a pair of wild boars."

"I thought you were sound asleep too."

"What, with you jogging your legs around like a jumping jack?" She laughed. "Honestly, Arty, mice and rats are pretty cute if you kept still enough to look at them. And let's face it – they're the only friends we've got here."

She joined him and they pushed their way through the loose panel in the tower, then went up the rickety spiral staircase. After several flights, they climbed out on to the roof.

Arthur balanced along the tiles and crouched at the end, taking in the view of Lontown. They could see everything from here. Around them were the Slumps, so accurately named with rooftops that curved and leaned precariously over the streets. Further north the houses were neater. Elegant shapes filled the skyline – the tower of the *Lontown Chronicle* and the huge domes of the

Geographical Society and Lontown Universitas. Despite everything that had happened, Arthur still felt Maudie would study at the universitas one day. She was destined to be the best engineer in Lontown. It was as though a shape which fitted her perfectly waited on the horizon. He thought he'd known his own destiny – Dad was going to take him on his first expedition. One day they'd build their own ship. Maudie would design it and the three of them would explore: Maudie as first engineer, Dad at the helm and Arthur as Dad's first mate. Now that future had been snatched away, and there was just a Dad-shaped hole in the world.

To the east, the river snaked through Lontown, and fog clung to the distant hills, seeping into the city. The moon painted a blue evening hue on the arched buildings of north Uptown. Thin twists of smoke rose into the sky all around and faint music floated towards them.

"Is that a banjo?" Maudie asked.

Arthur couldn't answer, his throat tight with sudden emotion. Dad used to play. Both of them stared in the direction of their old house, far off in the distance. Maudie took her mini uniscope from her tool belt and passed it silently to Arthur – their mother had made it and it was especially powerful, so they could see as far as their old neighbourhood.

Way in the distance, a warm glow shone from Arthur's old bedroom and the dark silhouette of a stranger could be seen. They had felt so free and so safe there. So happy.

"I can't believe there's already someone else living there."

"Arthur, it won't always be like this. You never give up on anything. You, me and . . . well, you and me against the world, isn't that right?"

He nodded. "Me and you."

"Come on, re-tie my ribbon with me." Maudie paused. "Although with the state of your hair lately, perhaps I should lend one to you!" Maudie ruffled her hand in his rusty brown hair. They re-tied her ribbon then Maudie got up and balanced her way along the rooftop to the clock face, climbed up and started examining the hand mechanism. Arthur remained where he was, watching a trade ship as it flew north across the sky not far from them, the faint chug of its engines carried on the warm breeze. Arthur watched it fly across the moon, leaving wisps of grey behind it.

After a minute he said, "We should get back."

Maudie didn't answer, and he couldn't hear her tinkering any more.

"I said, we should get back." He turned around and his heart stopped.

Because Maudie wasn't there.

Scrabbling to his feet, he leapt to where she had been and looked, desperate, over the edge, his head swirling with dread. "Maud!" he called.

"What are you shouting about?" she said, swinging around from behind the clock face, then jumping to land on the roof tiles beside him.

He thumped her arm. "I thought you'd fallen."

"Ow! I'm likely to, if you carry on like that! I was tweaking the mechanism around the back – it was out of rhythm."

Arthur gave her sleeve a tug as his heart rate slowly climbed down. "Come on, let's see what scraps we can find in the larder." As he stood, he felt compelled to have one last look back at Brightstorm House. He paused – a tiny shape now circled above it. "Pass me your uniscope, Maud." After a moment he said, "It can't be."

Maudie snatched the uniscope. "What is. . .? Oh!"

A pure white, moon-bright hawk circled the roof of Brightstorm House, its outstretched wings giving it a soft W shape.

Maudie lowered the uniscope and looked at Arthur, eyes wide.

"Parthena!" they both said.

Without needing to say another word, they scrambled down the tower stairwell and into the streets, running towards Uptown, hunger burning their bellies and their muscles on fire, but not stopping until they reached Brightstorm House. Wheezing, they stood before their old home in the moonlit square.

"What if Parthena won't come to us?" Arthur said. "She'd only ever land on Dad's arm."

"Try," Maudie said.

Arthur whistled a single note, like Dad used to. He'd left his iron arm back at Beggins Hall, so he extended his left arm. Parthena flew down from the rooftop, her flight path uncharacteristically shaky.

She landed unsteadily on Arthur's arm, her talons digging in. "It's all right," he said as Maudie stroked her. Parthena's grip softened and she dipped her head sadly. She was a large bird and filled the length of his lower arm, but she was so much thinner than when they'd last seen her many moon-cycles ago.

"She survived; she somehow made it back," Arthur said. Seeing her felt like having a little piece of Dad back. The bird had been inseparable from him: loyal for life, as all sapients were. They were rare in the Wide, so it was usually only explorers who came across them – or could afford the few being paraded in Lontown's markets, in the hope of a wealthy match.

"What happened, Parthena?" Arthur knew she could make sense of what he was saying. A sapient's heightened intelligence meant they could understand a person, but they couldn't communicate their own thoughts back easily.

Parthena screeched.

"It's all right, you're home."

"What's that in her claw?" Maudie said.

They both stared at it. An oval-shaped silver

locket was looped by its chain around one of Parthena's talons. Elaborately inscribed on the locket were the entwined initials V and E. Violetta and Ernest.

"It's Dad's locket," Arthur said.

"But how?"

Maudie gently opened it. There was the picture of their father smiling widely, slightly younger, his beard less full, his brow wrinkle-free. Beside him was a young woman with a hand placed lightly on Dad's chest, twinkling eyes and eyebrows set in a determined slant. The resemblance to Maudie was uncanny.

"Mum and Dad looked perfect together," Maudie said.

Parthena hopped on to Arthur's shoulder. His mind turned over and over, as he raised his arm to stroke her head.

"What are you thinking, Arty?"

"It doesn't fit. If Dad was being attacked by a great beast, how would he have had the time to take the locket off, give it to Parthena and send her on her way? That would hardly have been his priority, right?"

Maudie nodded. "And Parthena would have been fighting with Dad, until the end."

They both lost themselves in thought, standing alone in the dark street.

After a short while, Arthur said, "Maybe the locket means something more. And maybe they're wrong about what happened."

Parthena screeched.

Arthur and Maudie's eyes locked.

A spark of hope had lit inside Arthur. "I know it's a slim chance, but what if somehow he survived?"

Maudie shook her head. "Parthena wouldn't have left him."

Arthur took a few paces. "We have to find out."

"Arty, we can hardly traverse three continents without a sky-ship."

"There's always a way, Maud. We could go to the Geographical Society and show them the locket."

She paused for a moment then looked at him doubtfully. "They'll need some convincing it means something. They don't exactly think much of the Brightstorm name at the moment. They'll probably say we're making it up."

"Then what about the Polaris Challenge? You

heard Beggins say they'd launched another. We could go ourselves to find the truth."

Maudie laughed. "Now you're just being daft, Arty. We have no money, no ship, and that means no chance of going. Much as you can find a way around most things, I think you're dreaming."

"Remember what Dad said? Don't call it a dream, call it a plan. There's always a way, Maud, there has to be."

She sighed. "We should get back."

Arthur kicked his foot in the dust of the street.

Maudie put a hand on his arm. "Come on, let's think about it later. Right now, we'd better find a way of hiding Parthena, or Mrs Beggins will be selling her at Thimble Street Market on Saturday, or worse, have us cooking her for dinner."

They started making their way back to the Slumps.

A thin figure around the corner had been watching them. They didn't notice him slipping into the shadows as they belted past on their way back to Beggins Hall.

CHAPTER 5

POMERIAN PUFFBACK

Eudora Vane stared at the three hundred and sixty-five outfits in her great dressing room and the three hundred and sixty-five pairs of shoes lined up neatly below – one for every day of the year. If only they were good enough.

It wouldn't do.

Pomelroy Pompelfrey was late with her new set of outfits – was he going for an award as the most incompetent seam-master in Lontown, for guild's sake? She ran her fingers across a silk jacket. She couldn't address the Geographical Society board in one of these old things. She needed more funding – there was one thing she was certain of: sovereigns bred more sovereigns. It wasn't cheap being one of the most envied members of Lontown society, and this second expedition would take nearly everything she had. Fortunately, she knew it would be more than returned when she won the race to South Polaris – which she would, this time. But it was more than that. She wanted her statue in the Geographical Society's great hall of explorers, the next in the venerable lineage of Vanes.

An insect scuttled out from beneath the pink lounge chair and extended her four silver wings. She fluttered them and flew up to land on Eudora's finger.

"This won't do at all. I have nothing to wear, Miptera," Eudora said, then calmed her brow and cursed Pompelfrey for making her so cross. Wrinkles were very unbecoming. She made a mental note to send someone to retrieve more of the honeybloom extinctus, or whatever it was called, that was so good at soothing her skin.

Rushed footsteps stomped up the stairs and a bedraggled man burst through the door. He could barely be seen, due to the swathes of material in his arms – just two bloodshot eyes with bulging bags underneath, and a few tufts of hair on his balding head.

"Three days you've had since I rejected your last efforts," Eudora snapped.

Miptera took flight and hovered close to Pompelfrey, gnashing her silver mandibles.

"I'm sorry, Madame," came the seam-master's muffled voice. He gave Miptera a worried sideways glance as she lingered beside his face, the clack of her teeth growing faster. Pompelfrey's voice juddered. "Catching a pomerian puffback proved more difficult than one may expect, as there are but three left in the Wide."

"I hope you killed the other two, as well."

"I beg your pardon, Madame?"

"Good gracious, man – I may need matching accessories! And the one I wear would be much more desirable then, wouldn't it?" She rolled her eyes. Was the whole world really this slow? "Well – show me."

Pompelfrey heaved the many gowns across the chair.

He held up the first. "This is an exquisite silk

discovered recently. Made by indigenous people of the Eastern Isles, berry dipped and—"

"No."

He tossed it behind the chair and picked up the next – a lush pink fur. He'd hired five extra seam-masters to get right.

"No," she said before he could even begin.

He picked up the next – a tight-fitting bodice which bloomed out to a trumpet skirt with pink furry hems and cuffs. Pompelfrey's eyes were wide and hopeful.

Eudora tilted her head and reached to the plumes, so soft they could barely be felt. "Ah, the pomerian?"

Pompelfrey nodded.

She held it up – it matched her tall elegant silhouette perfectly. The board would give her whatever she wanted. "This one will do."

The edges of Pompelfrey's lips curled in a smile.

"But the pink needs lightening – see, the shade is out." She held it beside the three hundred and sixty-five others.

It looked identical to Pompelfrey.

"Have the dress back by morning."

Pompelfrey opened his mouth to complain, but he knew it was futile, so shut it again. "As you wish, as always."

"Don't use a tone with me, Pompelfrey – there are hundreds of seam-masters in Lontown queuing up for the chance to create for me. This will be front page in the *Lontown Chronicle*."

"Would six and thirty chimes suit you, Madame?"

"Make it six. And don't disappoint me," she snapped.

Pompelfrey dipped his head and Miptera saw her chance, darting in to bite him on the arm.

He yelped, and lifted his hand to knock her away, but managed to restrain himself.

"Now go. You've quite upset Miptera," Eudora said, waving him away. The insect landed on Eudora's shoulder, clacking her teeth triumphantly.

As a dishevelled Pompelfrey left the room, another man entered, tall and utterly calm in contrast. He took off his hat and inclined his head respectfully towards Eudora.

"Smethwyck, it's rather late for business – can't it wait? I'm meeting the board in the morning for the final expedition approval."

"This you will want to hear – I caught sight of a bird close to Brightstorm House."

She frowned, but quickly corrected it. "Hardly newsworthy of the *Lontown Chronicle*, Smethwyck." She threw herself back into the pink gowns on the chair.

"I'm certain it was Ernest Brightstorm's sapient bird, Eudora – the purest white hawk, not a marking on her."

Her eyes narrowed. "How could it have flown all the way back? When?"

"Not two chimes ago. The children got to it first. I thought you'd want to know," he said.

"Watch them closely and report back to me."

Smethwyck bowed and left the room.

CHAPTER 6

THE ADVERT

The Brightstorm twins hurried back to the Slumps, climbed the tower, crossed the roof, and sneaked back through the window to their tiny attic room. Parthena flew up to the exposed roof beams.

A loud growl came from Arthur's stomach. "Come on, the Begginses will be snoring away still – let's raid the kitchen. I'm starting to feel hollow and poor Parthena looks half-starved." Parthena gave a sharp screech. "Shush, Parthena. You'll have to be quiet here, we can't risk them finding you."

In the larder, the only food left on the work

surface was a lump of hard cheese, a crust of stale bread and half a boiled egg.

"Great, if it wasn't bad enough scrabbling around in their leftovers, there has to be an egg," Arthur said.

Maudie patted his arm. "Well, we don't want your tongue swelling like a ship's balloon so you can't talk." She paused. "On second thoughts. . ."

He pushed her shoulder jokingly. "I'll have the cheese. It should be fine if I cut off the mould." He opened the tap, then searched the cupboards for a clean cup while waiting for the pouring water to become less rusty brown. A spider scurried into the corner as Arthur took out a cracked cup. He couldn't help but imagine himself, Maudie and Dad back home in the drawing room with honeyed tea, buttery crumpets and sweet berry jam.

Arthur picked up the copy of the *Lontown Chronicle* discarded on the side. He read the headlines:

Pelt of vicious Third Continent Wolf makes
a record amount at auction

Blarthington drops out of bid for South Polaris after sky-ship fire

Labour urgently needed in southern pitch mines due to unprecedented demand

He tucked it under his arm, then they climbed the creaking stairs to their attic room.

Arthur threw the newspaper on to his bed and pressed his shoulder to the wall to undo his jacket fastenings. He wriggled free.

"What if Dad survived, Maud?"

"Arthur, we've spoken about this. We don't even have a sovereign to feed ourselves properly, let alone go looking for him."

Parthena flew down from the roof and landed on the *Lontown Chronicle.* She cocked her head and screeched at Arthur. "Parthena, you *must* be quiet."

Maudie took the crust from her pocket and gave half to Arthur with the old cheese. They nibbled in silence, feeding bits of bread to Parthena. Arthur stroked her pure white feathers – her beady eyes were so sharp and knowing. "If only you could talk," he said.

"He promised to come back," Maudie said sadly.

Arthur sat beside her. "He would've tried anything to get back to us." He wanted so much to put two arms around her and hug her, the way Dad used to envelop them both like a huge bear.

"I just feel so useless without him," she said. "Like I knew who I was, but now. . ."

"Dad told us Mum was the best engineer in Lontown, do you remember?"

Maudie nodded.

Arthur smiled. "You'll be a great engineer too. I mean, who makes an iron arm at eleven years old?"

Maudie arched an eyebrow, her mood lifting. "I was still ten, actually. And I'll make you a more powerful arm one day, with fingers that move with a twitch of your shoulder, so you don't have to even manipulate them into place with your other hand, and it'll bend at the elbow when you shrug. Dad said. . ." Quick as a gust of wind her face saddened again. "It's as though every trace of who we are has been wiped out, Arty. If I didn't have you, I would probably become invisible."

Arthur took the length of red ribbon from the

floor. “Remember what you started telling me almost as soon as you could put a sentence together?”

She looked at him.

“You said it didn’t matter that I had one arm, together we could do anything. We’re Brightstorms. Dad had to fight to be an explorer, the first ever in our family. He travelled all the way to the Volcanic Isles, through the worst storm the North had ever seen. But no matter how hopeless it became, he said there was a bright light he held inside: his determination to never give up. Against all odds, he made it, and discovered new islands and an amazing rare moth. So we’re Brightstorms, the name he chose for himself and for us.” Arthur held out the ribbon. “You’re Maudie Brightstorm, and one day you’ll be proud to say it again.”

Parthena screeched and hopped up and down.

“And you, Parthena. The last three Brightstorms against the world.”

Parthena scuffed at the paper with her talons. Arthur looked at the print at Parthena’s feet. He picked up the newspaper and a bolt of excitement rushed through him. A smile spread across his lips.

"What is it?"

He read aloud:

Individuals Wanted
For treacherous journey to South Polaris,
Small wages, certain danger,
Shared reward and recognition if successful.

Evaluations Monday
Apply to: Miss H Culpepper
4 Archangel Street

He looked across, eyes wide. "It's our chance, that's what."

Maudie frowned. "Arty, this is daft. We're barely twelve, she won't take us seriously."

"I read about her in the *Lontown Chronicle* – the youngest explorer to captain a sky-ship to the Second Continent."

"Not at twelve."

"But we'd just be part of the crew. With your engineering skills and my . . . well, I'm not bad in the kitchen now, and every ship needs a cook's help."

Maudie still looked doubtful.

"Come on, we at least have to try," he said.

"But Monday is tomorrow."

"Then we'd better think up a good excuse for the morning."

CHAPTER 7

LUCKY SPOON

The sun hadn't even peeped over the horizon when Arthur and Maudie woke. They sneaked downstairs and rushed through the morning routine of cleaning out the fireplaces and sweeping the floors.

"I can make up some excuse for the dock-master, but Beggins will know something's up when you're not there when she wakes," Maudie said, shutting the front door behind her.

"I'll say I went to Ratchett's to pick up her supplies. I can get them on the way back."

After a quick wash in the street pump, Arthur and Maudie headed north into the heart of Lontown with its domes, towers and great brick-fronted houses.

Eventually, they came to the street listed in the advertisement, Archangel Street. The houses were trimmed with ornate iron balconies threaded by rose-covered vines, arranged around a central square garden.

Maudie brushed Arthur's wayward hair through with her fingers. "We look like a pair of ragamuffins." Then she untied the ribbon and retied it around a wayward lock of her hair, holding it back from her face.

Arthur started up the street looking at the numbers: twenty, eighteen, sixteen, each one identical in its perfection. They carried on until they stood before number four.

He looked at the advert clutched in his hand, then up at the house. He frowned. "It looks as though someone jumbled up the pieces," he said.

Number four Archangel Street stood alone from the rest, and it looked unlike any building he'd ever seen. It was smart as its neighbours, with fine brass hinges on windows with polished frames, but it was crooked, as though the house insisted on doing its own thing. There were wooden panels with metal rivets, windows of different shapes, round and long and square, with intricate shutters on pulleys. Curious creatures were emblazoned in stained-glass windows at the top, and the whole roof looked as though it had been put on sideways.

"This is some house," he said.

"Wow, look at the mechanism on the windows! Some kind of auto-winder, by the look of it," Maudie said.

"Are you ready?" Arthur said.

She nodded.

Arthur's stomach turned over with nerves. He wanted it so much. What would Dad have told him? He remembered what he'd said before he'd left for the expedition: *Fear kills more dreams than failure ever will. You can be comfortable or courageous – never both at once.*

There was scuffling behind. Arthur turned and almost bumped into a rather round and tall woman stumbling off the curb. She cursed in the foulest language he had ever heard and a huge silver spoon fell from her coat.

Arthur bent and picked it up for her. He looked

at her curiously. The woman clutched a piece of paper the same as his. She wore a little tilted hat that looked like those the gentlemen of Uptown wore, and she had frizzy ebony hair. A heavily skirted coat bulged out like petals at the waist, and her enormous feet had been squeezed into what appeared to be gentlemen's brogues.

She took the spoon from him and smiled. "It's me lucky spoon, not that it's brought much luck today. Bleedin' shoes are four sizes too small. You'd think in the whole of Lontown I'd be able to get a pair in my size at short notice but, well, you'd think wrong."

"Yes, you would." Arthur nodded politely. He did his absolute best not to look at her extraordinarily large feet.

"Are you two here for the evaluation?" She looked at them with narrowed eyes and a knowing smile. One of her eyebrows raised independently of the other one. "Why, you look like a pair of scared bunnies."

Maudie smiled and said, "It just means a lot to us."

"It's a nerve-wracking business for sure, an evaluation, and one could easily turn from it at the last minute, like when I applied to go with the Acquafreedas on that expedition to the Island of Nimoy. I stood outside for a whole chime before I got the courage to go in. Mind you, I got the job and wished I hadn't because I had nothing to cook but bleedin' seaweed and spine fish for weeks on end, and they taste worse than a sea-sailor's stinky shoes, I tell you!" She took a big breath. "I vowed only sky-ships from then on, so as Granny said – if you want the best eggs go straight for the goose." She smiled. "I know! We'll go in together."

She talked a lot, but Arthur took an instant shine to her. "Thank you, but honestly, we're all right on our own."

She ignored him. "Felicity Wiggety, pleased to meet you." She reached for Arthur's right hand, looked down, then back at his face. "Oh! Will you look at that?" Her cheeks flushed beetroot. "Dreadfully sorry, sonny."

Arthur tucked the advert in his pocket and extended his left hand.

"I'm Arthur," he offered.

"Pleased to meet you, Arthur. Now there's a story behind that arm and no mistaking it, and I'm dying to know, but now's not the time to ask. It's something for friends to discuss, and as I've barely made your acquaintance..." Her cheeks blushed redder. "Brings a whole new meaning to putting your foot in it." She stared at her feet. "Ha! Putting your foot in it – me, who'd have thought!"

He could feel Maudie itching to give Felicity an arm story, but there was no way of getting a word in. Arthur and Maudie couldn't help but laugh.

"And this must be your . . . ah, a twinnie – a fine pair you two make, and no mistaking. Like popples in a pod, matching freckles and dimples to boot! I can tell we're all gonna get on," she said, hooking Arthur's arm. "After all – I'm footloose and fancy-free and you're completely 'armless!"

She put her hand over her mouth, clearly shocked by what had come out, but Arthur grinned. It felt good to make light of it; most people looked at him with alarm, as though his situation was contagious, or worse, they looked at him with pity.

As Felicity paused to take a breath, Maudie saw her chance. "He was struck by lightning twice in one day, in a storm in the Northern Isles. The first bolt took his hand, the next his elbow."

Felicity laughed. "Ha, what a yarn, no mistaking."

Before anyone could say another word, she escorted them up the steps.

Underneath the number four on the wall, a brass plate read *Aurora Heights*.

Dad had told Arthur a story about the aurora. Strange magical lights of all colours which appeared in the furthest skies.

"Go on, one of you knock," said Felicity.

"You do it, Arty," said Maudie.

The painted black door had a great brass knocker in the shape of a bird; Arthur thought it was a swallow. He lifted it and let go, the loud knock echoing in the street.

After a moment, slow footsteps approached, and the door creaked open. An old man with collar-length white hair combed neatly backwards surveyed them from top to bottom. "Can I help?" he said, his voice raspy, with the poshest Uptown accent. He raised his V-shaped eyebrows.

"We're here for the evaluation," Maudie said.

As he dipped forward, his whole body curled over them. "You're children," he said curiously.

Arthur looked up. "We're twelve and two moons."

The butler shook his head, then gestured to Felicity. "This is very irregular. Just the Madame, I'm afraid."

"Look here. . ." Felicity waved her hand.

"Welby," he said, giving the faintest dip of his head.

"Welby, this is my niece, and this is my nephew. Hugely knowledgeable they are in ship-like affairs. I completely vouch for their talents in. . ." She looked to Maudie.

"Engineering," Maudie said proudly.

Felicity gave an impressed nod. "And. . ." She looked at Arthur with an encouraging smile.

All he could say was, "Er, knives, in the kitchen."

Felicity swallowed and raised her eyebrows. "Yes, knives, such a talent. So, where I go they go. Besides, it says open evaluations, ain't no age specified – give them a chance, will you?" She grinned toothily.

Welby surveyed them, a small amused grin on his lips. "I suppose you'd better come in, then."

CHAPTER 8

HARRIET CULPEPPER

The hallway was grand, with russet star-shaped tiling on the floor. Lamps dangled from the ceiling at different heights, giving a warm glow to the wood-panelled walls filled with drawings of exotic landscapes. The scent of spices hit Arthur like a blow to the chest – it smelt of home.

Welby moved slowly, every step considered, as though his joints had rusted. He showed them into a large empty drawing room off the hallway. Blossom petals drifted in from an open door at the far end.

"Queenie will tell you when it's time," Welby said. With a nod he slowly left the room.

It was a peculiar room with enormous hinges in the corners of the ceiling and pipes twisting in and out of one of the walls, as though the parts that were usually hidden had broken free from inside.

They listened to the groan of Welby's footsteps heading up the stairs.

On a chair opposite, an enormous fluffy cat stared at them, her fur the colour of stormy clouds, especially thick around her chin. She observed them with intelligent amber eyes and flicked her velvety tail. "I'm glad we left Parthena at home," Arthur whispered.

The walls of the drawing room were as full as those in the hall: cabinets and cases overflowing with shells, skulls, jars, feathers, pinned butterflies, rocks and drawings of weird and wonderful creatures.

Shortly, the cat's ears pricked up, then the creaking of stairs sounded, and the front door opened and shut again as someone left. The cat jumped from the chair and stood in front of Arthur and Maudie. "Prroah, miaow," she said.

"I guess this is Queenie," Arthur said.

"I think she winked at you," Maudie said, blinking.

"Meowt," the cat said.

"I think her intention is to say *what are you waiting for*?" Felicity whispered.

"She must be a sapient animal," Maudie said.

Arthur nodded. "She certainly seems pretty clever."

"So I guess you follow her."

Queenie looked to Maudie. "Meowt prrwt."

"I think she means both of us." Arthur squeezed Maudie's hand.

Felicity wished them luck as they followed Queenie out of the room. Every stair creaked as they walked. Queenie led them to a door at the top of the stairs and meowed. Arthur paused, then knocked.

Maudie had become fixated on a lever imbedded in the wall. "Look at this, the chain goes all the way through the wall – possibly a signalling system to the kitchen," she whispered.

Arthur wasn't listening, he felt too nervous. Footsteps approached from the other side. His stomach churned.

The door creaked open and Welby surveyed them. "If you could refrain from touching anything," he said. Maudie quickly took her hand away from the lever.

A bright, yet serious, voice came from deep in the room. "Welby, show them in."

He stepped aside and gestured for them to enter. Arthur and Maudie tiptoed into the dimly lit room. Fringed lamps dotted the many tables lighting an explosion of paper, books and small machinery. A young woman sat at a large table at the far end of the great room, head down, scribbling with a feather pen. She dipped the nib in a pot and, without looking up, said, "Names?"

"Maudie."

Arthur opened his mouth but nothing came out. Maudie pushed his shoulder.

"Arty... Arthur," he said.

The young woman behind the table looked up at him. She couldn't have been much more than twenty-five, with short, ruffled hair that wanted to go in different directions and eyes that sparkled with life and fire as though fuelled by some sort of magic within. They reminded Arthur of Dad's. Her gaze lingered on Arthur's iron arm.

"Maudie and Arthur...?"

"Just Arthur."

She nodded and scribbled some more. The sound of the pen scratching filled the room. Welby took a seat to the side of her.

"And why are you here?" she said.

"Well, we…" Arthur started but his throat jarred.

She nodded encouragingly.

Maudie continued. "We saw the advertisement in the *Lontown Chronicle* and…"

The young woman stood and walked around the table to lean against it. She wore baggy trousers tucked into knee-high leather boots, a loose shirt and a curious belt with lots of dangling metal instruments. Arthur glanced at Maudie, whose eyes had widened and fixed on the tools.

The woman shook Maudie's right hand, then Arthur's left. He caught sight of two small birds in flight tattooed on her wrist. They were explorer marks. Every notable explorer used their family symbol – Dad had the mark of the Brightstorm moth. Arthur had been fascinated with it as a child and had made Maudie draw one on his wrist in ink that washed away within days.

"Swallows are the bird of freedom," she said, catching Arthur's eye. "My name is Harriet, just Harriet, or Harrie to my most trusted friends, or Harriet Culpepper if you'd really like to know, or Harriet Mildred Audrey Culpepper if you're from the bank, and here on official business." She leant in teasingly and winked. "Which you're not, are you?"

Welby coughed. "They're very young."

Harriet put her hands on her hips. "So was I on my first expedition – it didn't stop me." She cupped her hand to her mouth and stage-whispered, "Welby's been with the family for ever – he's my second in command. He'll be the first to admit he's no spring chicken, but he's surprisingly nimble, and quick thinking in life-or-death situations."

Nimble wasn't the first word Arthur would have thought of.

"So tell me about yourselves," Harriet said brightly.

"I work in the shipyards," Maudie said.

Harriet tilted her head and nodded.

"Maudie can fix anything," Arthur said.

"I'm an engineer, like our mother," Maudie added.

“Interesting. . .” Harriet said, leaving it hanging for a moment, something clearly turning over in her brain. “And do you sing?”

“Do we what?” they said in unison. They used to sing all the time – Dad would play the banjo and they would sing old explorer songs together.

Harriet smiled. “Not to worry, Welby sings well enough for all of us – very important on an expedition, you know.” She paused, the curious look back in her eyes. The silence felt suffocating by the time she said, “So won’t your parents miss you?”

Maudie cleared her throat. “Mum died when we were born and Dad. . .” She looked at Arthur.

Harriet stared deep into his eyes, a quizzical bend to her brow. Then she nodded as though confirming something to herself.

“An expedition really is no place for children,” Welby persisted.

Harriet waved his comment away. “Expeditions are all a matter of motivation. My dream is to be the first to lay my feet where no human in this world has ever reached before – quite simply to see if I can.” Her eyes twinkled. “The sovereigns will, of course, be a bonus, but it isn’t everything. So my question to you is: why do you want to leave the life you have right now?"

Silence hung in the air.

Arthur cleared his throat. "We've always wanted to explore. We know we're young, but—"

Harriet interrupted. "Honesty is the foundation of a good crew. I want you to tell me what is *really* motivating you."

He felt as though she could see right inside – that she somehow knew. Maudie gave him a small nod.

"Our father was Ernest Brightstorm."

To his surprise, Harriet didn't look taken aback; she simply said, "I read the news with interest, of course. A terrible business."

"He wouldn't have stolen the fuel," Maudie jumped in.

"I was going to say it was a terrible business being attacked like that, by beasts." Harriet left a long gap. "The Geographical Society agreed there was no other explanation for the theft of fuel from the *Victorious*."

"There was no real proof. What if it was local thieves?"

She tilted her head. "So your reason for wanting to come on my expedition?"

Arthur swallowed. "Our name has been dragged into shame. All we ask is for a chance to reclaim it by succeeding and reaching South Polaris."

Maudie stepped forward. "We're not afraid of getting dirty and pulling our weight – we'd work twice as hard as any other member of your crew."

Arthur took over. "We'd do everything we can to help get you to South Polaris first."

"Arthur might only have one arm but it's strong as two, and he can problem-solve a way through almost anything because he's always had to. You should see him tie a knot, and he's great in the kitchen, and. . ."

Harriet let out a small laugh. "OK, I get it." She considered them for several seconds more. "It was a pleasure to meet you both." She shook their hands and returned to her desk and picked up her pen. "A very good day to you."

Welby shuffled forward, ushering them towards the door. "We'll be in touch if you are successful," he said in an unconvincing tone.

The door closed.

So that was it. They'd failed. They hadn't even been asked for their address. They slowly, dejectedly descended the stairs.

Felicity came out of the drawing room. "How did it go?"

Arthur shook his head.

"I'm sure it wasn't that bad, dearies. I have a tingling in my toes and sure as anything that means the wind's changing."

"She couldn't get rid of us fast enough," Maudie said.

"Come now, you must remember ... there's always hope." Felicity winked at Arthur.

"Unfortunately hope has developed the habit of abandoning us lately, but thank you for your kindness, Miss Wiggety. I hope you have better luck than we have," Arthur said.

CHAPTER 9

AN OFFER

As the days passed, the tiny attic room of Beggins Hall seemed to shrink around them. It rained constantly, and they couldn't keep up with mending the leaks in the roof. Parthena took shelter inside with them, but their few possessions were crammed into the corner, and with one mattress too soggy to sleep on, they squished together on the other and fought over the scratchy blankets.

"Let's go. There's no sense in just sitting around here for a message that won't come. Come on," Arthur said.

Maudie took a deep breath.

"What is it?"

"Maybe we should face the facts. We haven't heard from Harriet Culpepper."

"The official start is tomorrow morning, there's still time. Let's go down to the dockyard. Maybe we can stow away on her ship. Or someone else's!"

"It's getting too close. We need more time to plan."

"We have to do something."

Maudie looked down and twisted a ribbon in her hands. "Perhaps we have to come to terms with the idea that we may never know the truth about Dad."

"I can't believe you're saying that!" Arthur couldn't accept it – he never would. "We'll find a way. Dad sent the locket back because it means something and we need to find out what." He hated when they argued because it made him feel the threat of being left alone. She was the only one who truly understood him, especially with Dad gone.

"But I don't see how—"

There was a tap on the window.

"Arty, it's Queenie!" A great fluffy face pressed against the glass. Maudie opened up the window and the cat leapt inside. "There's something around her neck." She unclasped a silver tube from

Queenie's collar and carefully removed a rolled-up paper from inside.

The cat gave a satisfied "Prrrrwt".

Parthena screeched angrily, but Queenie turned up her nose, jumped back up to the window and padded nonchalantly away across the rooftop.

Maudie opened the scroll and read:

Dear Arthur and Maudie,

I'm pleased to offer you both positions as crew-members on the Trans-Continental Expedition and Race to South Polaris – Arthur as cook's help and Maudie as second engineer. The Geographical Society has set the challenge to start at 8 chimes, promptly, tomorrow. We will depart from No. 4 Archangel Street. Please take extra care until departure; there have been a series of curious incidents and accidents affecting other ships.

Yours with faith,

Miss Harriet Culpepper

Arthur's heart raced. Harriet wanted *them* on her crew. They were really going! "This is it, Maudie." He felt he could explode with happiness. He whooped and danced around the tiny attic room. Maudie giggled.

"Brightstorms!"

They froze.

"Get yourselves down here!"

Arthur stuffed the note in his pocket.

"Come on. At least we won't have to put up with this much longer," Maudie said.

"Not even she can spoil my mood." Arthur smiled.

They ran down the stairs, and heard voices coming from the dining room.

A sickly sweet scent wafted towards them, some sort of botanical perfume, but it was unlike the scent of flowers in their old garden or the blossoms at Archangel Street. They slowly opened the door.

A woman, dressed from head to toe in pale pink, stood beside Mrs Beggins, a distinctive silver brooch on her jacket. Every inch of her seemed perfect: the cut of her skirt and jacket, the precision of her cheekbones, the small sweet nose, her silky braided hair and perfect rosebud lips. It was Eudora Vane.

"If you could let me speak with them alone, Mrs

Beggins?" she said, her voice soft and slow, and as sugary as the scent carried on the draught.

Mrs Beggins flushed red, flustered to be in such company. "Of course. Madame, if I'd known you were coming I would've made the lazy blighters work twice as hard to get the house clean. Just let me know what you need the little miss to mend on your ship and we'll arrange terms." She gave a nod, sovereigns almost replacing her eyes.

After the door closed, Madame Vane indicated for them to sit. She sat herself opposite and neatly clasped her pink-lace-gloved hands. "My name is Madame Vane," she paused and smiled, "but why don't you call me Eudora."

Arthur frowned at Maudie. What could she want?

Eudora Vane's explorer tattoo showed on her wrist – a beautiful winged serpent clutching a ring. On the bottom a small flying creature, identical to her brooch, clasped a rose.

"Pardon me, Madame Vane. But what can we do for you?" Arthur said.

Eudora Vane smiled. "I told Mrs Beggins that I needed some work on my ship and was looking for young workers to help, smaller crew who can reach further into the holds. I said that I must speak to you confidentially, on account of the secrecy I require on all matters pertaining to my ship." She winked.

"You want us to work for you?" Maudie said curiously.

Eudora Vane shook her head. "No, I'm not in the business of employing children to do my work, like some in the shipyards. Or those dreadful pitch mines! What happened to your father and his crew was terrible. Believe me when I say I understand how awful it must have been for you. When I discovered you had lost your home, I just had to find you." Her eyes roamed around the dark room. "It took me a while to track you down. What a despicable act by your former housekeeper to abandon you." She leant forward. "And then I heard that you had responded to Miss Culpepper's expedition advertisement."

"How do you know about that?" Arthur said.

"Word gets around in explorer circles."

"We. . ." Maudie started, but Arthur nudged her under the table.

"Don't worry, I won't say a thing to these dreadful people," Eudora Vane whispered. "But do you really think your father would have wanted you to follow in his footsteps and risk your lives?" She paused. "I understand you wanting to get away from your situation, but I've been thinking, there must be more to it."

Arthur thought for a moment. He couldn't see the harm in telling her, maybe she could help. "Dad's hawk, Parthena, flew all the way back, and she brought his locket, a locket he never took off."

"A hawk! A sapient, then? Curious indeed. So you think there is more to what happened out there?"

Arthur shrugged. "Maybe."

"We saw the prints of beasts in the snow; there were no survivors. I can assure you, we checked the area thoroughly," Eudora Vane said with conviction.

"He couldn't have sent it back in the middle of an attack."

"So you think he somehow survived."

"We know the chances are slim, but. . ."

Madame Vane leant back in her seat. "Conditions down there are harsh, Arthur. And as you say, his hawk never left his side, so by your own logic she wouldn't have left him while he was alive."

She was right, but it still didn't fit.

"I know you both want to cling to some shred of hope – we all do – but perhaps the bird found this locket after the attack and somehow made her own way back."

Arthur didn't want to hear any more. "We should be getting on with our chores."

"Please, I want to help you – I can pay the rental of a small house on the edge of Lontown. It would be all yours. I can find you both respectable work where people needn't know your name or heritage and you won't need to answer to anyone. Perhaps in the seam-master houses of Westside – they're always in need of young apprentices. I'm very well connected down there."

"Excuse me, Madame Vane. But why would you help us?" Maudie said.

"Because what happened isn't your fault. And an expedition is no place for children."

"We're twelve and two moons," Arthur said. While the idea of a warm place and security was an offer they might never see again, Arthur felt the weight of Dad's locket against his chest. He looked at Maudie. He didn't want to give up.

Maudie sighed. "Thank you, but we can't accept your offer," she said.

Eudora Vane gave a gentle nod of acceptance. "I understand. But at least think about it."

She stood and walked to the door, then paused. "Oh, there is one more thing. Miss Culpepper's attempt is rather naïve, I'm afraid. She may appear exciting, quite the young explorer, but she has no experience of the Third Continent. She doesn't even have a worthy sky-ship. She's hired quite a miserable thing, I'm afraid. If you don't believe me, you should go see it for yourselves – the *Sojourn*, down in the docks. I've been preparing and adapting *my* ship for another attempt since I returned."

Arthur and Maudie couldn't help exchanging a panicked look.

"The *Victorious* is far better equipped for the journey than any sky-ship in the First Continent. I would say that with my recent modifications it is indeed the best sky-ship Lontown has ever seen. Perhaps I could show you one day, if you accepted my offer."

Maudie's eyes were bright with interest.

Eudora's gaze settled on Maudie's hair. "What a lovely ribbon – I should give you one from my own collection, something with a softer hue to it. I adore beautiful things and textures: fur, feathers, silk." She sighed. "So you'll think about my offer? It might be your ticket back to Lontown society."

A warm bed in a non-leaky room in Westside sounded like luxury, but Arthur knew he could never be happy, no matter where he was in Lontown, not until he'd tried to find out what had really happened.

Eudora read the expressions on the twins' faces and seemed resigned. "Independent spirits – I admire that." She opened the door, and stepped out into the hall before turning back. "I felt it my duty to offer you a way out. You understand, don't you?"

"We really do appreciate your offer," Arthur said.

"I set off in the morning, so you'll need to act quickly. Come to Vane Manor by seven chimes this evening if you want to accept; if not, I'll assume you aren't interested." She smiled graciously, then left.

Her sweet perfume lingered in the room.

Arthur was quiet for a while before saying, "You

weren't thinking of taking her offer of help, were you?"

Maudie paused, then shook her head.

"I mean, trying to tell us Harriet's not got a worthy ship!" he said.

They both let out a nervous laugh then fell silent.

"If Harriet really does mean to use the *Sojourn*... Well, I have seen it down in the dockyards, and it's not very big. Or well-maintained... It's a bit of a wreck, really. Although maybe Madame Vane was misinformed? We could check, to be sure," Maudie said.

Arthur took the note from his pocket and nodded. "Let's finish the chores, cook dinner, then sneak back to Archangel Street. We can ask Harriet directly about the ship."

CHAPTER 10

TRUST

After dinner, they made their way Uptown and knocked on the door of number four Archangel Street.

After a while Welby answered, one bushy eyebrow raised. "You're quite early."

"May we speak to Miss Culpepper?"

"She's not here."

"Is she preparing the sky-ship?"

Welby frowned.

"It's just..."

"Someone told us..."

"That, well..."

"It's the *Sojourn*, down in the docks. And it's a bit on the small side," Maudie finished.

Welby leant towards them. "And who told you that?"

Arthur's cheeks flushed with red. He didn't think he should mention Madame Vane.

"Expedition relationships are based on trust. I sincerely advise that if you don't trust Miss Culpepper, that you consider not turning up tomorrow. Good day." Welby began closing the door.

Arthur stopped it with his foot. "But..."

Welby tilted his head. "But nothing. Trust, or do not. Be here at this door by eight chimes tomorrow, or not. The choice is yours," he said, and shut the door.

"That was strange," Maudie said.

"What do you think?"

She shrugged. "Remember what Madame Vane said? We need to let her know by seven chimes. I don't know, Arty, maybe we should..."

Arthur took the locket out. "Maud, Harriet Culpepper has given us a chance we may never have again. We have to take it, even if it all goes wrong tomorrow and her ship is a disaster, and we have to stay at Beggins Hall for ever. I'd rather take the risk than never know."

He pulled her away and they began walking back to the Slumps.

Shortly, a clock tower bell began to chime. They paused and counted seven.

"So, this is it. We're really going with Harriet Culpepper," said Maudie.

He nodded. "Come on, let's get back to Beggins Hall. We can leave early in the morning – we'll be long gone before they realize."

They dashed along. Arthur was too wrapped up in the thrill of what lay ahead to notice the figure in the sharp suit watching them. As they walked through the alley on the way back to Beggins Hall, he struck.

Arthur saw the flash of a white handkerchief, and smelt the bitter tang of chemicals, then everything went black.

*

Arthur awoke to darkness and a familiar sound, yet his brain couldn't make sense of it. He felt for Maudie beside him, grasped her elbow, and groaned.

His head throbbed and the insistent noise was making it worse. In fact, the sound was making the whole building shake – a curious, slow bell. He remembered the handkerchief.

A grunt came from Maudie. "Ugh, I feel like I've been in a stampede," she murmured.

"Where are we?" He tried to open his eyes but everything blurred.

"Stop the chimes, Arty, they're making my head explode."

Chimes! He recognized them as they stopped – the low bells of the old ship watchtower in the Slumps, *their* watchtower, had rung a quarter to . . . *something*, directly above. He couldn't be sure the number of chimes. Warm morning light shone beneath a distant door. He realized they were in the cellar. His stomach lurched. The light meant it was already the next day – the start day of the expedition. They were miles away from Archangel Street – he could only hope they weren't too late.

Maudie seemed to think the same thing, as they both sat bolt upright in panic.

"Sis, we've got to get out of here." Arthur

scrambled to his feet, which made his head bang even harder.

"But what if someone's guarding us?" Maudie whispered.

"Come on!" Arthur clambered up the steps. He looked under the door. "I can't see anyone."

Maudie yanked the handle furiously. "Is anyone there? We're locked in!"

Arthur banged his hand against the wood. "Hey!"

"Help!"

Arthur nudged Maudie to the side and started pulling at the handle.

"It's not going to suddenly open for you, is it?"

"Don't snap at me, Maud!"

"Why have we been taken? Who would do this?"

Arthur thought about the rumours of children being taken from the Slumps to work in the pitch mines. "We've got to get out of here before whoever it is comes back!"

"Look, yanking a handle isn't going to get us anywhere. Search the room for anything that could help us out." They ran back down the stairs and began scrabbling around on the dusty floor and feeling the walls.

"There's nothing," Arthur called. But there had to be a way – there was always a way.

He ran back up the stairs and began examining the door. "These hinges are as old as this building. If we can prise the pins from them, maybe we could lift the door right off."

The pins came out easily enough, but as they grabbed on to the wood to pull it open, the bolt on the other side stuck fast. They could only get it open an inch or two.

"We need something to lever it open," Maudie said.

"I know, but we don't have anything!" Arthur snapped.

"Arty."

"Shh, I'm thinking."

"Arty."

He shook his head and kicked the door, panic rising with every passing second. "We're not going to make it in time."

"ARTHUR!"

He stopped and looked at her.

Raising her eyebrows, Maudie said, "Your arm."

He squinted at his sister for a moment then

seemed to realize what she was suggesting, just before she explained.

"I'll pull the door back as much as I can – then you put your arm in the gap and lever while pulling with your real hand."

He nodded. "On three – one, two. . ."

They pulled with all they had, and a sharp slither of bright morning light cut into the cellar.

"It's not wide enough!"

"Pull harder!"

They grunted with the effort and the gap widened just enough for Arthur to push his iron arm through. "Keep pulling. I'll wrench it open," he said.

The wood groaned with the strain and the rusty bolt on the other side of the door creaked.

"It's not budging." Arthur's metal arm began denting under the weight of the door.

"Don't ease up, give it everything we've got – brace your foot on the frame. Together."

With one more mighty effort, there was a creak and a ping, and the cellar door flung inwards, sending them crashing backwards.

"We did it," Arthur said in a muffled voice from beneath the door.

"Great, and we're a lot flatter."

Kicking the heavy wood out of the way, they saw the cellar was flooded with daylight. They jumped up and dashed from the watchtower into the street outside, right into Mrs Beggins, sending her empty basket skittering across the cobbles. She grabbed them roughly by the scruff of their shirts.

"There you are! What do you two think you're playing at?"

CHAPTER 11

WHAT GOES UP

Mrs Beggins yanked them closer, shaking them with firm, pudgy hands. "You blighters didn't come back last night. What have you been up to?"

Arthur looked at the tower clock. It was a quarter to the chimes of eight.

"Mr Beggins!" Mrs Beggins shrieked.

Mr Beggins came running out of Beggins Hall.

Arthur knew they didn't stand much chance of escaping if Mr Beggins reached them too. He exchanged a quick look with Maudie. Each of them stamped hard on the nearest foot to them. Mrs Beggins cried out in pain and let go.

The twins pelted along the street and turned into Old Ropey. The Begginses' footsteps thundered behind them. As they took a turn into the tight alleyway of Sankey Row, Mr and Mrs Beggins' shouts weren't far behind.

"There they are!"

"Get them, Mr Beggins!"

With a great screech, Parthena swooped into the alley ahead of them, urging them forward. They ran onwards, knowing if they gave anything less than one hundred per cent it would all be over. Their lungs burned, yet on they darted through the alleys and streets as the minutes passed too quickly, towards Archangel Street, their leg muscles on fire.

Not knowing it was possible to run any faster, they sped through the last few streets as the o'clock chimes rang across Lontown.

One . . . Two . . . Three. . .

"Come on!" Arthur called. Four . . . Five . . . Six. . .

Seven. . .

They rounded the corner to Archangel Street as the eighth and last chime sounded.

A crowd gathered before number four. The ground rumbled. Everyone gasped.

The house was doing something utterly extraordinary – the front seemed to be folding inward, revealing great pistons and cogs, whirring and crunching. Then the edges of the house joined at the front – the door had entirely disappeared inside. Shutters opened beside the windows and small propellers sprouted from the house, unfolding and turning.

With the scrape of metal, and a sound like a great cog clunking and grinding, the roof lifted backwards, folding in a huge concertina.

As it peeled back, Arthur could see Harriet Culpepper close to the front above, standing by a great wheel. Her short hair waved in the wind; she wore flying goggles and a white scarf billowed beside her. Welby was close by, pointing and ordering the others who had gathered on the roof. Felicity Wiggety was there, her cheeks red and giant spoon in hand, waving at the crowds below.

The cannon sounded at the Geographical Society, signifying the start of the challenge.

"Wait!" Arthur called desperately, but his voice was drowned by the further rumble of engines from deep inside the house. As the previous roof disappeared over the back, a great cloak of white fabric expanded above into an enormous balloon. Ropes were being pulled and tied and extended and heaved. Arthur watched, his mouth wide, utterly amazed at what he was seeing, but his heart pumped with panic.

There was a great tearing sound and the crowd took several steps back as the house lifted and ripped clean away from the ground.

Then came a shout which made his blood turn to ice.

"There they are! Stop them!"

Arthur looked over his shoulder to see Mrs Beggins pointing, doubled up. Out of breath, she had collapsed to her knees, but Mr Beggins was heading straight towards them.

Arthur and Maudie pushed on into the crowd.

The commotion hadn't gone unnoticed above. Felicity leant over the side shaking her arm. "Arthur? Maudie? Bless my soul, it is you!"

Mr Beggins grabbed Arthur's left arm and twisted it behind his back. "Now where do you think you're escaping to, boy." Maudie lunged, but he was too quick and grabbed her around the neck.

"Let go of her!" Arthur shouted.

Then Parthena dived from the sky, claws bared for Mr Beggins. She grabbed his hair. He let out a yelp, but managed to hold on tight to Arthur and Maudie, who were still panting from the run. Parthena flew upward again.

The house rose higher as the balloon above grew ever bigger. Clunks and motors sounded as more sections of the house curved and changed, slotting into place. Number four Archangel Street was unlike any other house because the rickety patchwork building had hidden a great secret: it was also the most extraordinary flying ship.

Finally, a small section of wood above creaked and revolved. It revealed a shining bronze plate which read: THE AURORA.

As the ship rose, Arthur's stomach sank further to his feet. Mr Beggins's hot breath was in his ear, his left arm pulled painfully against his back. Above, Felicity waved her chubby arms and Harriet Culpepper was now beside her, frowning, while Felicity pointed furiously at Arthur and Maudie. Harriet shook her head and said something to Felicity, then turned and disappeared. Arthur's heart stopped – it was too late. They'd missed their chance with Harriet.

"You didn't think you were going with them, did you? You're a nobody. Who else in Lontown would take in a good-for-nothing, broken boy like you? I paid good sovereigns," Mr Beggins sneered into his ear.

"Sovereigns that we've earned back many times over," Maudie shouted.

Then, a flash of silver came from above. The people standing either side of Arthur stepped aside, but Mr Beggins was too busy trying to keep hold of the Brightstorms to notice. Felicity's great spoon spun through the air and hit him square on the forehead. His grip lost power, and he fell to the ground with a great thud.

"You've got to be the foulest, kid-crunching, spindly worm I ever set eyes on, picking on innocent children." Felicity Wiggety blew a great raspberry.

Maudie gasped for breath and rubbed her neck.

"Are you all right?" Arthur said.

She nodded. "Of course, are you?"

"Never better."

Felicity cheered and beckoned them to hurry.

The ship hovered a good two metres from the ground now and started to rise.

Harriet Culpepper appeared once more beside Felicity, but this time she held a rope. Her eyes met Arthur's. "You can do it!" she called, then hurled the rope into the air – it fell just short of the ground. Arthur felt every eye in the square on them.

"Jump!" Felicity shouted.

Maudie jumped first and scurried up the rope to make room. Arthur ran toward the rope as it rose along with the ship.

"Come on!" Maudie cried.

With an almighty leap he propelled himself up and grabbed the rope with his left arm. Within seconds his muscles burned. He twisted his wrist and wound the rope around.

"Don't you dare let go, Arty," Maudie yelled from above, but there was little he could do, as he couldn't clamp his iron hand on to the rope without the other hand moving his iron fingers. He would have to hold on, or it would all be over. Gasps came from the crowd as the ship rose. When he glanced down, Mrs Beggins was there, jumping for his foot, grabbing it. With every bit of energy he could gather, Arthur kicked out of her grasp and she fell backwards. Arthur slipped down, only just managing to keep a hold. A second rope fell down alongside him as the ship ascended at an alarming rate. His heart plummeted to his boots as he rose up and up.

"Don't look down!" Felicity shouted.

"Hold on," called an approaching voice, strong and commanding; Harriet Culpepper was climbing down to them on the second rope. "Keep going up, Maudie – I'll help Arthur."

Every muscle in Arthur's left hand and arm burned furiously, and the straps of his iron arm dug into his shoulder, pulling at him.

Harriet shinnied down beside him. "Can you swing your legs and wrap them around my back? We'll go up together."

"I can't clamp my iron hand on the rope without using my other hand. I can help pull with one arm if you can take my weight?"

"Don't worry about that – the crew will help us. Swing over on three, squeeze tight, let go of the rope and grab my shoulders. One. . . two. . ."

"You can do it, Arty," Maudie shouted.

Arthur swung his legs towards Harriet. For

a dizzying moment, he looked at the crowd and his weight dragged him back. They gasped and screamed, and Parthena dipped and whirled around him, unable to assist. Then he released the rope and threw his arm around Harriet, trying his best not to strangle her.

She glanced over her shoulder at him. "Good, now hold on tight. Pull us up," she called.

When they were level, Maudie began climbing alongside them.

At the top the crew hauled them all over the edge. Arthur and Maudie collapsed to their knees on the deck, gasping for breath. Then they looked at each other and laughed.

"Whoa, when Mrs Beggins jumped for you!"

"I know! Did you see?"

"And then you went back and—"

"I nearly fell!"

"You held on!"

"You were a natural!"

"And Miss Culpepper!" they finished together, looking up as Harriet climbed over the side and jumped to standing, as though she'd simply been for a stroll around the garden.

"That's one strong arm you've got there." Harriet adjusted her scarf. "I take it you both accept my offer of employment?"

The twins nodded and grinned.

"Then welcome aboard the *Aurora*." She put her hands to her hips. "But I should be clear that lateness will not be tolerated."

"Sorry," Arthur said.

"Captain Culpepper," Maudie finished.

"Captain Culpepper was my father. I built my ship with a different philosophy in mind: we are all in this together, and we'll have to take on different roles throughout this journey, so titles have no place here. It's the strength of our ideas that will give us authority, not a title we bear. So please, call me Harriet."

Parthena screeched and Arthur extended his arm. She landed gracefully, then butted her head into his cheek.

"And you're welcome along too, although I'm not sure Queenie will be pleased," Harriet said.

A shout of "Watch out!" came from below, followed by the flash of silver and a clang as the spoon clattered across the deck.

"It's me lucky silver spoon!" Felicity raced to the edge and looked down. "Thank you, people of Lontown!"

The metal spoon nearly came to a stop a few inches from Arthur's iron arm, then changed direction, gliding over and sticking against the metal. He pushed himself up and lifted his arm and the spoon towards Felicity.

"How in Lontown are you doing that?" Felicity said.

"It's magnetized," Maudie said proudly.

"Bless my bunions, you clever thing!" She laughed.

"But I hate to tell you, it means your spoon must not be silver after all," Maudie said.

Felicity frowned. "But Great Uncle Mungo swore it was forged in the silver mines of Berick Barr, the lying lizard!"

Maudie shrugged awkwardly. "Sorry."

Footsteps clunked across the deck. Arthur recognized the highly polished shoes of Welby. "You obviously chose Madame Wiggety for her language and charm," he said to Harriet, in his polite Uptown tone.

"Despite her salty language, her chocolate cake is legendary in Lontown," Harriet said. She smiled and shrugged.

Welby looked at Arthur and Maudie. "When you two have finished having fun, we've got a ship to steer. And after that little delay, our rivals are already much higher than us."

"Then all crew to the pumps!" declared Harriet, her cheeks glowing and an undeniable sparkle in her eyes.

CHAPTER 12

THE AURORA

There wasn't a moment to recover. After squeezing Arthur and Maudie into a tight hug, Felicity tugged them both over to the port side of what had once been a rooftop and was now the ship's deck.

"What in Lontown's sails happened to delay you?" she said.

"Someone locked us in a cellar," Maudie said.

"Good gracious."

"We don't know who."

"Everyone, to your posts!" Harriet called.

"Best talk later," Felicity said.

The *Victorious* was visible above the docks a

short distance away, rising powerfully into the sky, its wings spread majestically wide. Another sky-ship rose beside it, dwarfed in size. Then another caught Arthur's eye further west. A fizzling knot of competitiveness formed inside him.

"Turn! Turn!" Welby shouted rhythmically from the other side.

Arthur threw all his energy into turning the cog. The great fabric balloon grew bigger by the second and a judder came from the engines below as something fitted into place. Then a repeating *whirr, clunk* sounded like a great heartbeat.

Harriet Culpepper stood at the wheel, her hair and scarf flowing messily in the wind. She looked ahead through her binoscope. "Good work," she called. "Get those sails fully open – we need more lift, to aid the balloon."

Great connected cogs with handles ran along the inner edges of the deck. Half of the crew lined each side. Maudie took the handle in front.

The sun, due east of the city, was a glowing peach rising over the ridge. Below, the houses and streets had become miniature, like a child's wooden model.

"Move the cogs or we'll end up crashing into one of those towers and it'll be the shortest expedition in history!" Harriet ordered from the central wheel.

"Put your backs into it," Welby called from the other side.

Felicity patted Arthur on the shoulder. "Focus on the cog – it's just like stirring Granny's stottle cake – that mixture was deadlier than a glue bog. C'mon, Arthur, we can do this. You just swung one-armed from a flying house; anything's possible!"

"Come on, port side – push harder," Arthur shouted along the crew line.

Behind him, Maudie was encouraging the other half to turn faster. The cogs gained momentum, then there was movement and a flash of white to the sides. Great sails began extending from the *Aurora* into view of the deck. It was beautiful, like the wings of a bird unfolding for their first flight. Parthena gave a screech of approval. She flew above them, gliding effortlessly on the wind, showing them how it was done. The *Aurora* lifted; the *whirr-clunk* of its engine heartbeat slowed a little. Glancing over his shoulder, Arthur saw the *Lontown Chronicle*

Tower just beyond the Geographical Society, getting closer by the second. The other ships were already higher than them, the smallest ship shooting into the lead, followed by the *Victorious* and the others. They passed far above the dome of the Geographical Society, then over the *Lontown Chronicle* Tower.

"Don't stare. Keep turning!" called Harriet.

The wings were halfway out when Arthur's arm jarred and machinery groaned. The sail had jammed.

Harriet ran to look over the side of the ship. "The sail's stuck in the extender," she said, as though it was a mere inconvenience, while the tower loomed closer and closer.

Arthur felt certain they wouldn't make it.

Without a thought, Harriet jumped up, then did a forward somersault through the air, landing with absolute precision on the edge of the wing.

Arthur swallowed a big gulp of air.

"Oh my, what if she falls!" said Felicity.

Harriet scampered along the wooden spine towards the end of the half-extended wing.

"If she doesn't sort this out, we're done for!" said one of the crew members.

The entire crew stared wide-eyed as she sat balanced on the edge, wrestling with the mechanism.

Suddenly, her arms flew backwards as the sail came free and the momentum propelled her back. The crew cried out in alarm, but Harriet reacted quickly and regained her balance. "The mechanism is released," she called as she hurried back along the wing.

Felicity erupted with applause. "Bravo!"

Arthur raised his hand to Maudie's, and together they clapped.

"No time for celebrating! Make haste, crew! Back to the cogs!" Harriet shouted, staring at the approaching tower. "And work like your life depends on it, because it does!"

"Yes, Captain," the crew responded.

Both sides of the ship wound the cogs furiously, and after a minute a firm *clunk* travelled through the deck. "Starboard sail open," Welby called.

"Come on," Felicity said from the other side. "Last push, everyone!"

Arthur put everything he had into it, until his shoulder burned and muscles cramped. After one huge effort, a rumble vibrated the deck as the port side sail extended into place.

Harriet Culpepper was back at the bow, legs planted, hands firmly clasped on the handles of the enormous wheel. Queenie leapt across the top as she turned it. The shadow of Parthena stretched as the ship tilted.

"Everybody hold on! Clip in your safety rope!" Harriet called.

Anything loose began rolling across the deck of the ship.

"Hope you've got your air legs on, twinnies," Felicity called. Her voice was carried away on the wind.

Arthur realized he wasn't secure and stumbled as he reached for the handle of a cog. His hand still felt numb from the pumping and he missed. Before he knew it he was slipping down the deck. He stopped suddenly as Felicity grabbed hold of his belt and pulled him back and clipped a safety rope to him. They tilted even more, to a heart-stopping angle. Arthur's stomach turned.

"I keep telling you, don't look down." Felicity laughed a huge hearty laugh and whooped at the top of her voice.

Queenie, who was surprisingly agile for her size, remained balanced on the wheel in front of Harriet.

The tower was now only seconds away. Other buildings whizzed below, alarmingly close.

"Are we going to crash?" Maudie shouted, her eyes wide and terrified.

"Not on your nelly. Hold tight," Felicity called.

There were several alarmed shouts as they neared. The great sails missed the building by a whisper.

Every member of the crew looked behind as they passed out of harm's way, rising higher and higher. The *Aurora* levelled, and the crew collapsed in a grateful heap on the deck. Harriet laughed. "What a start!"

Maudie turned to Arthur. "I've got to examine the engine and the wings. The mechanism is genius," she said, her eyes wildly keen and excited. "And there's something different about the engine; it doesn't sound like they normally do."

Arthur smiled at her. He'd not seen her so happy since before. Since Brightstorm House.

He looked over his shoulder to Harriet, who had her binoscope fixed on the *Victorious*. Eudora Vane's ship seemed to have travelled twice as far as they had in the same time and powered ahead with a thick black trail of pitch smoke chugging from two huge outlets. The smaller sky-ships had only one outlet each, but followed not far behind.

"The smallest ship looks like the *Fontaine* original!" Maudie said.

"I didn't know they were making a try for South Polaris."

"Which means the other is probably the Bestwick-Fords. Everyone else must have dropped out."

"Ours is by far the best-looking ship," Maudie said with a smile.

Arthur had to agree. Their balloon was streamlined, the wings as graceful as Parthena's, the woodwork perfection. He put his hand to his iron arm. "We're on our way, Dad."

Felicity joined them. "Right – I'd say we deserve a nice cup of tea."

*

They flew through night and day across the rolling hills of the lower lands of Lontown, passing over small towns and buildings clustered below, patchwork fields, and farms. At first, they could name the villages: Dreyton, Summerville, Bifflewick, but the further away they flew, the harder things became to recognize. On the second day, they passed over Chesterford, the second largest city in the First Continent and the furthest Arthur and Maudie had ever travelled before.

The weather was fine. As time went on, Arthur kept checking the binoscope to see if they were gaining any distance. They remained close to the small *Fontaine*, and the *Victorious* and Bestwick-Ford sky-ships remained visible through the binoscope – always ahead on the horizon leaving their dark trails across the blue, like dirty roads in the sky. Harriet carried on in her steady, sure way, un-panicked by the fast progress of the other ships and the increasing gap between them.

The first week was filled with the rigorous learning of procedures. Life as cook's help meant Arthur spent lots of time below deck with Felicity in the *Aurora*'s galley. It was non-stop with fifteen crew members to feed. He could peel an apple in seconds, thanks to the spring-mechanized clamp

Maudie made for him, and her spike board helped him chop vegetables even without his iron arm. At first he had worn his iron arm all the time, unsure of how the crew would react, especially after his experience with the Begginses, but he soon learned that every member of the crew had a kindly nature and nobody stared or made awkward comments.

By the end of the week, he still couldn't remember every crew name, but they all had a role and Harriet insisted everyone take a turn assisting another crew member to learn new skills, in case anyone fell ill or had an accident. He'd particularly liked helping Meriwether, a smiley young meteorologist, and Gilly the enthusiastic, curly-haired botanist, who told him stories of rare plants and animals he'd found on his last expedition with Harriet to the East Insulae.

Carried on a favourable wind, by the eighth day they'd reached the border of the First Continent and the fens, where they stopped for the night to refresh the engines. Harriet ordered complete rest for the crew and insisted on cooking while everyone came together to eat on the deck, watching the sun set across the marshy land, orange light shining between the reeds.

Maudie had found out everything about the engine in the first week. "It runs on water – can you believe it? Harriet Culpepper is a genius. Forbes told me about it in the engine room. Apparently, Harriet's parents were great inventors too. But water, Arty! Clean, efficient fuel, not like the smelly pitch other ships use – it's nothing short of inspired. The idea stemmed from something the people of the Second Continent are developing for irrigation."

"Sounds impressive," he said. But he wasn't truly paying attention; he was thinking about what lay ahead. He didn't particularly care about how the ship worked and how they got there, as long as they did.

"I know you're not really listening, Arty. But you'll be interested in this."

"I was listening," he protested.

"Sure you were." Maudie shook her head. "Well, the clever thing is Harriet's been developing the water engine technology for two years, all in secret – I spoke to the crew second-mate, Hurley, and she said if other explorer families had known, they would have stolen her technology. Think about it, Arty – sea ships have been restricted by the dangerous waters surrounding the Third Continent and some other parts of the known Wide. Sky-ships are limited by the amount of pitch they can carry and where they can get supplies. With a water engine, anything is possible! Adapting a house that could become a sky-ship was the perfect cover. And by renting that small decoy ship at the docks, nobody even realized what she was up to!"

Arthur smiled. It was a brilliant idea.

That evening, as they took off from the shores of the First Continent, a great weight lifted from Arthur; they were really starting the journey towards the truth. The Culldam Sea stretched endlessly ahead. Arthur wondered how anybody ever discovered land beyond it. Everything looked so much bigger than in the maps. Dad had told him that the first explorers from their continent to reach the Second had travelled in sea-bound ships, before sky-ships were invented. The first sea-ship sailors felt they'd gone so far, they were sure they'd gone full circle when they finally landed, until they realized they'd only crossed the Culldam Sea and had actually discovered a whole new continent.

The next morning Arthur awoke before anyone else, when it was still dark. He got up, trying his best not to make his bunk creak, and put on his trousers and shoes. Leaving his iron arm by his bed, he then sneaked along the hallway and up the stairs to the deck.

The breeze was silk against his skin and the *Aurora* flew beneath a cloudless sky, a dark blue sheet pricked with thousands of tiny lights. He could even see the shape of the galaxy in an arc overhead – millions of dense bright speckles, together unimaginably huge, and himself beneath it an insignificant dot on a flying ship. Yet he felt so connected with the sky, as though for that moment they were the same. He wondered if one day sky-ships would be invented to fly even higher, above the mountains and into the deep sky – he imagined Maudie engineering a ship to take people to the stars themselves.

"What are you up to?" Maudie suddenly

appeared behind him. But her voice faded as she became entranced by the sky too.

He grabbed her sleeve and tugged. "Come on – let's walk on the wing."

"Arty, seriously?" she said, but was already laughing and following him to the port side. "I'll go first," she said, pushing in front.

"No way, it was my idea," he said, pulling her back.

They edged their way down the small rope ladder used for maintenance, crawled along the edge of the wing, then sat and swung their legs around so they dangled below. The sea was almost invisible, just the odd glint of reflected light. They put their fingertips to the sky and felt the breeze dance around them. The distant east was brightening to shades of light blue and orange. Parthena screeched three times from the side of the ship, then took flight. She circled them, and as a sliver of sun rose, she spun in the air in front of them. Arthur held his arm out like a bird's wing and Maudie did the same on the other side. For the first time in many moon-cycles, nothing seemed to matter.

When Arthur eventually looked back over to the ship, he saw Harriet leaning on the side, watching them. His heart jumped, as he expected a stern word, but she simply said, "My parents used to hate me doing that." She smiled, then turned away, checking her compass.

CHAPTER 13

THE LIBRARY

As the days passed, there was a place on the ship that Arthur and Maudie loved most of all, and they sneaked off to it in the free time allowed every evening after dinner. The *Aurora*'s library was a small room with wooden shelves from floor to ceiling and all the books were about geography, science, exploration history and engineering. Felicity had added some of her own: *Rare Herbs of the Northern Marshes*, *Lontown Broths*, and her favourite – *One Hundred Teas from Afar*. Maudie was already on the second shelf of engineering books and was reading *A History of Ship Aviation* by Corinthia Strunk, while Arthur was devouring the books about history, many of the same titles that had been in their library at home, but he never tired of them. To see them again felt like finding a little piece of home.

Today, one particular book caught his eye, a journal that must've been the notes for *Exploring in the Third Age – a Potted Overview* by Ermitage Wrigglesworth. Every word was handwritten and the illustrations meticulously drawn. Mr Wrigglesworth was a revered academic expert on everything explorer related. Arthur turned the pages with delicate precision, making sure he didn't smudge any. There were little additional notes scribbled in the margins with extra facts that he couldn't remember having read in the printed copy in the library at home, and Arthur lapped up the details. He turned to the section with notes on *Explorer Families of the Third Age*. The directory was in alphabetical order, starting with the Acquafreeda family, then the Aldermysters on the opposite page. The name Acquafreeda was beautifully scrolled and beside it was a drawing – their explorer family symbol. It was a huge, fat fish, and each scale had been beautifully rendered. To the side was a description of the family traits and characteristics:

Legendary and master handlers of sea-born ships
Usually quiet in demeanour yet characteristically bold (especially in the water)
Value all things seaworthy and of the sea

He read on to the section on the page marked *History.*

The Acquafreedas were the first explorers to ever take to the sea in the Second Age of Exploration. Their legendary crossing was to the Western Isles of Carrickmurggus (the most significant step since the discovery of the route through the Northern Marshes at the end of the First Age of Exploration). The Acquafreedas never took to the invention of sky-born ships at the dawn of the Third Age of Exploration, and while the family remains active in exploring, they mainly concern themselves with exploring down rather than out, and spend much time researching ways of travelling beneath the water itself (a much frowned-upon and often laughed-at exploit which has lost them some credibility over the years).

Arthur looked over at Maudie sprawled on the floor, her nose an inch away from her book.

"This explorer family wants to explore underneath the water, Maud – imagine..."

"Fascinating," she said dreamily as she snapped her book shut and took another from the engineering section. The shelves had become littered with strands of ribbon, marking the pages Maudie was most excited by.

Arthur read on. After the "A" family pages came the Bafflewiffles, the Bestwick-Fords, the Blarthingtons, Bottomroys. He flipped the page quickly to the Cs. There was no mention of the Brightstorms in this book – they were too new to the scene. The usual route to becoming an explorer meant being born into a wealthy explorer family in Lontown. But their father had broken the mould. Arthur remembered the piece of paper in his iron arm that had been torn from the book. At least their family had made it into one book, and it gave him comfort to know the image of the Brightstorm moth was there, as though their father was somehow travelling with them.

He glanced over the next page, which was the Catmole explorers, whose symbol was a cat with a tail curled into a question mark. He rushed through their family history, then flipped the page, knowing what was coming next.

Culpepper.

He traced his fingers over the two birds, facing each other, dipped in flight but with eyes meeting. They were so life-like and intricately drawn. He'd never wanted to stare too long at Harriet's tattoo – it seemed impolite – but now he could study the details of the feathers and the aerodynamic shape of the wings, which now struck him as identical to the shape of the *Aurora*'s wings. He read the characteristics:

Loyal and True
Inventive
Bold

It was so simple, much more so than the others, yet it summed Harriet up perfectly. He read on:

The swallow tattoo is a symbol for everlasting love and loyalty to the family. Swallow pairs, native to the northernmost lands of the First Continent, travel long distances, only to find their way back to each other at home.

"That's beautiful," he whispered.

"Hmm?" Maudie said, again in a tone which meant she still wasn't listening.

The Culpeppers were one of the first to venture the enormous distance across the sea to the Second Continent. Before their expeditions, the family name was Culpiper, but was adapted with the discovery and return of the rare peppers and spices from the Second Continent which are commonplace in Lontown Society today.

No wonder the maps of the Second Continent he'd seen on the ship were so incredibly detailed.

He carried on through the explorer names, and

by the time the sun dipped on the horizon through the small portal window of the library, he had almost reached the end of the alphabet. Although he was squinting to read, he didn't want to stop to light a lamp because the next name was Vane. He remembered seeing Madame Vane's family symbol when she'd visited them in their attic room. Now he could see the details of this strange creature. A serpent with claws clutching a suspended ring. At the bottom of the ring was a rose and inside the ring, on top of the rose a great winged insect was poised. It was a strange mixture of something strong and beautiful. He read the characteristics:

Kind
Courageous
Wise

The adjustable vane-like tips of the wings give the serpent absolute precision in flight and the ability to out-fly smaller prey. One of the most long-standing explorer families in Lontown, their reputation was made with the discovery of the East Insulae, where the precious and valuable pink dye (in Lontown known as Rosea) originated from the huge, endangered beetles named the Rosa Scarabaeus, found living on one of the islands.

He looked at the symbol again – there was something bothering him about the illustration, but he couldn't work out what.

Maudie tapped his shoulder and he jumped. "Come on, you can't read in this light, and Welby will be looking for us if we don't do the evening checks soon."

He placed the green ribbon in the page and put the book back on the shelf.

"What are you frowning about?" Maudie asked.

"Something; I can't put my finger on it."

At that moment, Welby whipped the door open and dangled his pocket watch before them.

"We know," said Maudie, pulling Arthur along the corridor. Then she whispered, "That man can sure say a lot with his eyebrows."

CHAPTER 14

THE EXPLORER'S JOURNAL

The following afternoon, Felicity taught Arthur to make egg-free marsh cakes. As soon as Felicity had found out about his allergy, she'd begun creating all manner of foods free from the ship's store of egg powder. The marsh cakes were her latest experiment and were green as the North Swampland because of the pinch of bog herb, and a strange mix of sweet and savoury.

Arthur munched as he looked through the large binoscope on the bow, scanning the horizon. He could see the *Fontaine*, but the other two ships were out of range.

"Boo! Made you jump!"

Without looking up, he passed Maudie a marsh cake. "No, you didn't; I heard you coming a mile off."

"Ew, this looks weird."

"Trust me, you'll want to try it."

She took a reluctant nibble and a huge smile broadened on her face. "Have you got any more?"

He passed her another. "Why didn't you come to the galley for elevenses?"

"Harriet was showing me how to lock in the turbine for a water change."

"Riveting." He yawned dramatically.

"It *was* riveting, actually. At least fifteen rivets along the engine block seam." She punched his iron arm so it rang.

He shook his head and smiled, then focused on the distance again.

"Can you see the others?

"The *Fontaine* isn't far ahead."

"What about the Bestwick-Ford ship?"

"It's actually called the *Fire-Bird*, after a mythical bird of the East. They claim to be the only humans to have encountered one. And no, I can't see it."

"And the *Victorious*?"

He shook his head. "Long gone."

"Don't worry about that," she said knowingly.

He put the binoscope down and looked at her. "Why?"

"Well, if you paid any attention to the things I try to teach you..."

"Tell me and I'll give you another marsh cake."

Maudie smiled. "It's the type of engine power each ship has. The *Fontaine* is small and Harriet says it will never make the crossing to the Third Continent. She said the two smaller ships are naïve about the distance they need to cover. Also, the Bestwick-Ford's *Fire-Bird* has triple engines and is what Forbes calls 'a right pitch guzzler'. Eudora Vane's ship is big and fast, and she also relies on heavy amounts of pitch to drive her pumps, but her stores are bigger. So far, the *Victorious* has been pushed hard, to get ahead of the competition. I've completed the calculations." She pulled out a piece of paper with scribbles and symbols all over it.

He shrugged. "It's like a different language."

She tutted, tugged him towards the wheel, pulled a map from the stand and spread it on the deck. She pointed to Lontown. "Here the *Victorious* is fully loaded with fuel. She's heavy and pushing her engines to full power, so she's speeding off ahead, but still within our sight."

Arthur nodded.

"When they reach the Culldam Sea they've burned half their fuel. They're much lighter, but their engines are still running at maximum, so they are going even faster." She whooshed her finger across the sea to the Second Continent. "Based on size, capacity, estimated weight, speed and so on, at the rate Eudora is pushing the *Victorious*, they'll need to refuel in the Citadel of the Second Continent. The *Fontaine* and *Fire-Bird* will have to refuel before that and they'll soon fall behind. From the Citadel, the *Victorious* will push on to this point of the Second Continent, the Last Post, and refuel again if they can, so they'll be heading across the Silent Sea on a full tank. Are you following?"

"Surely this is bad news for us? With a full tank, they'll speed across the Third Continent." He ran his finger across the great white expanse and stopped at the area marked *Unknown* where huge mountains were in a semi-circle around an enormous frozen lake.

"Right – except you're forgetting one crucial thing."

Their eyes met. "What?"

"They've got to make it back. There's no pitch to buy in the Third Continent. They'll have to cut their speed as they advance or they'll burn their fuel store too quickly and be stranded."

"Ha, right! You're a genius, Maud."

"Not really, Harriet helped me. I've calculated they'll have to halve their speed, which means we'll catch them up and take over right about. . ." Maudie ran her finger across the map and then tapped on the area on the Third Continent. "We maintain the steady pace, take over and reach the great frozen lake of the Third Continent first – that's as far as anyone has gone before. Then we find a way to get past the shard mountains. Harriet has a secret idea, based on how the Vane expedition described the mountains in their report to the Geographical Society. She suspects they may be a certain type of ancient volcanic formation with tunnels that cross through, much like the ancient volcanic islands in the north, known as the Big Four, which she explored a few years ago. We travel *through* the mountains and get to South Polaris first!"

"But doesn't the water of the *Aurora* engine need changing? What if we can't make it back and all the water is frozen over?"

"So, you *have* been listening," she said with a satisfied smirk. "We're heading across a land of snow, but the frozen lake is full of cracks and shifts. We'll send our pipes down into one of the gaps, so water won't be a problem."

"Oh, of course," he said.

"Why are you two snickering so excitedly?" said Felicity. She tottered across the deck and set down a tea tray rattling with china cups and a teapot. "There you are, my poppets." She took a handful of marsh cakes from her apron and put them on the tray. Maudie quickly grabbed two, then looked a bit sheepish and handed one to Arthur.

Harriet left the wheel to another crew member and joined them, followed by Queenie, who curled up at Maudie's feet and purred happily while Maudie stroked her chin. Parthena swooped from the sky and landed on Arthur's extended iron arm.

Queenie hissed at her, then went back to purring. Parthena gave an irritated screech.

Harriet laughed. "Perhaps they'll grow on each other!"

"It's funny, Arty, but Parthena always chooses to come to you, just like she did Dad."

Arthur smiled. It somehow made him feel closer to Dad.

"So, forgive the pun, but have you brought your brother up to speed?" Harriet said.

Maudie nodded.

Taking a pencil from behind her ear, Harriet drew an X on the edge of the area marked Everlasting Forest. "This is about where we'll set down when we reach the frozen lake. The last expedition reported a great semi-circle of mountains, impassable by sky-ship because of the close density, sheer faces and height – the balloon can't take the expansion at that altitude."

"They make the northeast mountains of the First Continent look like babies," Felicity added, taking off her great shoes and wiggling her toes in the sun.

"So that's where Dad's ship might still be?"

"We may certainly pass it, although who knows

what the elements will have done to it." Harriet put a hand on his shoulder.

Felicity poured the tea. "Sweet and strong for what's ahead, dearies."

"By Maudie's calculations, if the wind is favourable, we should reach there a day and a half ahead of the *Victorious*." Harriet smiled and walked her fingers across the frozen lake to the mountains, as though it would be the easiest thing.

"Oh, I nearly forgot. I have something for you, Arthur." Harriet took out a brown leather book. "I thought this could be your explorer's journal. Every expedition must keep rigorous records, and it's good training to get you into the habit."

The Culpepper swallow symbol was embossed in silver on the front. Arthur smiled and ran his fingers across it. "Thank you, Harriet."

"Our priority is to reach South Polaris, of course, but I want you to write everything about the journey so far, and continue to record thoughts and observations as we progress, as well as a record of our journey. It could prove useful in a trial back in Lontown, if your father's case gets reopened. You never know what might prove to be important later."

Felicity clapped her hands together. "Well, this is exciting. I knew the moment I read the papers something didn't fit. I felt it in my feet, you see." She turned to Harriet as though it needed explanation. "It's a tingling sensation I get across the sole when things aren't right. Like if I bake a bad muffin."

Harriet laughed.

"I don't think you could ever bake a bad muffin!" Arthur said.

Felicity's cheeks flushed like the rising sun and she smiled widely. "Always room for improvement, I say."

"Not with your cooking, Miss Wiggety; it really is the best in Lontown," said Harriet.

Felicity wiggled her toes.

Harriet passed Arthur her pencil. "Maudie, if you can check the water levels, and Arthur, write as much as you can before we reach the Citadel, which won't be long – I see a line on the horizon."

They rushed to the side of the ship. Below, the sea twinkled with sunlight, and ahead a thin band of russet coast, the first thing they'd seen other than water and sky in two weeks – the Second Continent.

CHAPTER 15

DESERT SANDS

They landed on the rusty red coastline of the Second Continent and replenished the water for the turbines. After so long in flight, it felt strange to be on solid ground once more – Arthur's body still wanted to sway with the undulations of wind and air. He looked around in wonder at the strange, warm, rocky landscape surrounding them. He bent and picked a handful of the gritty reddish-brown sand and the thrill of being somewhere new rushed through him, taking him by surprise. He'd been so intent on thinking about what may have happened to Dad, that he hadn't allowed himself to properly enjoy the idea that they were also on an expedition. Every day had brought new, amazing sights, and the more he saw, the more he wanted. The Wide was so much bigger than he'd ever imagined.

Not wanting to lose any time, the *Aurora* soon took flight again. As they flew inland, the rocky coast gave way to vast green plains. From time to time, they saw clusters of round white huts with roofs piping smoke through the tops. Groups of people rode together on horseback, herding cattle and sheep. There were patches of forest where Arthur caught sight of wild boar. Sometimes Harriet flew the *Aurora* low, and members of the crew would throw down sweets made by Felicity to the sun-blushed children who ran below them on the green open spaces, waving, smiling and calling up to them. Further south were rocky outcrops populated by herds of goats, great curled horns crowning their heads. Arthur saw some on the sheer rock faces, scurrying up as easily as if the steep walls were flat on the ground.

Two days into the Second Continent, they passed the *Fontaine* heading back north. The returning ship sent over a carrier pigeon with a note: she had a damaged propeller and had sustained a leak in the fuel tank and needed to make repairs that would be too costly in time. They would just make it back to the coast then would need to sail their ship the old way, over the Culldam Sea.

"One down, two to go," Harriet said when they'd continued.

Over the next week, Harriet flew them further south, veering a little to the west where she showed them stone dwellings in the hills. They stopped briefly at a place called Dueldor – a city over a thousand years old, entirely carved from soft stone. Everybody lived in caves with small windows in the hillside. Some of the people were wary, but Harriet could speak the language as though it was her own, and they were soon welcomed. They replenished their water from the great city wells before flying onwards.

Over the coming days, the land became drier. They saw a creature that Gilly the botanist identified as a sand bear, a slow lolling beast meandering peacefully across the land. There were certainly fewer people in the Second Continent than the First, and many more animals roaming free than on farms in the towns around Lontown. They saw fewer settlements over the desert plains, but Harriet explained that was because the conditions were tough mid-continent and most lived in the Citadel further south, where the plains ended. They were heading there to fully replenish supplies and stop for an evening meal. Arthur was pleased, as no dinner onboard meant he had some free time in the late afternoon – and the heat had become unbearable in the galley.

Arthur lounged on the deck in the shade of the balloon, welcoming the slight drop in temperature and the breeze. He watched Harriet at the wheel as Welby scanned the horizon with the binoscope.

"I can't spend another moment near the engine. If Cranken or Forbes come looking for me, tell them I died of heatstroke," Maudie said, collapsing beside Arthur.

"It won't last. Felicity says a storm's coming. She felt it in her toes."

"Well, who could argue with that?" Maudie looked doubtfully at the cloudless sky.

"I think Welby's sun-baked into a statue. He hasn't moved for the last five minutes," Arthur said.

But at that moment, Welby called to Harriet, who joined him. He gestured below and they swapped the binoscope between them a couple of times.

"What do you think they've seen?"

"Right now, I'm hoping it's a block of ice the size of a city." Maudie yawned.

"I'm going to find out." Arthur pushed himself up and sidled close enough to overhear what they were saying.

"Drop altitude, we need to get lower to be sure," Harriet said.

"We shouldn't stop until the Citadel, Harrie. If we get involved in business that's no concern of ours, it could delay us – we have a tight schedule, and Cranken says the water in the engine is evaporating at an alarming rate in this heat."

"Hush, Welby, you know very well that if there's someone in trouble down there we have no choice but to help, whatever that does to our expedition schedule."

Welby turned to give Arthur the one-eyebrow raise.

"Sorry, I didn't mean to sneak up," he said.

"Really?" Welby's eyebrow arched even higher.

"Here, Arthur. What can you see?" Harriet handed him the binoscope and pointed to an area below.

"There's someone, I think they're waving, but they look distressed, and . . . Harriet, I don't know if I'm seeing what you are, but I don't think they've got any legs."

"Take the ship down," Harriet called across the deck.

They began a rapid descent, and landed the *Aurora* in the sand a short distance from the figure.

The whole crew rushed to the edge.

"We can't stop here long," Forbes said, shaking her head. "The sand will play havoc with the engines and we need to make sure we can take off again."

"Have some compassion, Forbes," said Felicity. "We'll just help this poor soul, and take him to the Citadel. We won't be long."

Now they were close, Arthur could see that the poor man was not legless, but he was trapped in the sand from the chest down.

"Lower the gangplank!" Harriet ordered.

Deckhand Barnes wound the great cog and the plank began extending towards the sand.

Arthur stood poised – the poor man looked terribly distressed. Before the plank reached the ground, Arthur had run down and was belting towards him.

"Stop!" Harriet yelled. "I think it's quicksand!"

Arthur halted just as his feet slopped into the gluey mixture. They began sinking, and he just managed to hop backwards. The rest of the crew disembarked the *Aurora* and rushed to join him on the sand just short of the danger. The man yelled in a foreign language and flailed around frantically. He began sinking even deeper. Arthur went to take a step and reach towards him, but Maudie pulled him back and glared at him.

"But he's going to drown in the sand, Maud! We can't just watch him."

"You'll be stuck too, if you're not careful, then we'll have two people in trouble."

Harriet began calling out in what sounded like the same language as the man's and making gestures with her arms and legs.

The man began following her instructions. He pulled his chest forward and, after a while of wriggling as Harriet continued shouting out instructions in the foreign language, his legs lifted behind him. The man's eyes looked panicked and kept flitting about. As he crawled towards the edge and was pulled free by deckhands Keene and Forsythe, something caught Arthur's eye on the sand dune behind.

A figure dressed from head to toe in sandy robes, rose from the dune before them, throwing off the beige blanket which had concealed him.

Arthur pointed. "Hey!" he called.

Then Gilly shouted, "Over there!" as another rose to the left, then another and another.

There was a strange moment of frozen bewilderment as the crew watched the figures rise, then Felicity shouted, "We've been tricked!"

There was a clunk behind and Arthur turned to see a stranger on the deck, furiously winding the cog to pull back the gangplank. "Someone's on the ship!"

"Maudie, you're fastest – come with me! Hold the rest at bay, crew!" Harriet called as she rushed back towards the *Aurora* with Maudie. "Whatever you do, don't let those men make it to the ship!"

Arthur's heart pounded in his ears as he attempted a tally of the bandits heading towards them from the dune. The numbers seemed quite even, but the assailants held weapons.

He looked over his shoulder to see Maudie reach the gangplank, closely followed by Harriet. They pulled themselves up, but the figure on deck grabbed a broom and began jibing it so that they couldn't go any further. Harriet was shouting at him in the strange language.

The gang from the dune stalked nearer, spreading wide like a big net about to enclose them. Arthur spun around looking for anything that might help.

"Don't you have any weapons?" he said to Welby.

"Harriet doesn't believe in them."

Arthur let out a groan of disbelief.

"Neither do I," Welby added.

The glint of light reflected off what looked like a curved sword in one of the gang's hands.

"Trust us, Arthur."

"I have a weapon," Felicity said, brandishing her lucky spoon. "I told you a storm was coming. These feet are never wrong."

"I was hoping you meant the rainy sort."

Beside Felicity, Gilly rolled up his sleeves to reveal his not-very-ample muscles. It wasn't looking good.

Two of the bandits suddenly broke into a run,

scooting around the quicksand and flanking the crew on either side. One charged towards Felicity and Gilly. Felicity yelled and swung her lucky spoon in defence, striking the knife from his hands. But Arthur didn't see any more, as in a flash the other bandit was heading his way. Arthur braced, but Welby stepped in front of him, and in what Arthur could only describe as a bizarre series of arm twists and leg lunges, he'd disarmed the man and had him down on the floor, the man's own knife pressed to his throat.

Arthur looked behind him to the *Aurora*, desperate to see if Maudie was all right. To Arthur's relief, Harriet had somehow jumped on to the ship and was now wrestling with the man at the cog. There was a crack as Harriet hit the man and he fell to the deck.

Distracted, Arthur had forgotten the man they'd saved. Two hands grasped Arthur's shoulders and flung him into the quicksand. In his terror, he struggled and threw himself around, but the more he tried to get free the more it sucked him in. Everywhere he looked, the crew was busy wrestling and fighting with the attackers. Arthur was alone in the sand, sinking, trying with every inch of his body not to panic, and failing. His iron arm had yanked upward in the fall and rested on the quicksand, but he knew it wasn't enough to stop him sinking. Each time he tried to lift a leg up, the suction pulled it back in. And not only that, the crew were losing – the attackers now had Barnes, Forbes, Cranken, Gilly, Forsythe and Keene on the ground, surrendered at knifepoint. Now Meriwether, Dr Quirke, Wordle, Hurley and Felicity were outnumbered and one bandit had taken her lucky spoon and was laughing. A shadow passed above and Parthena released a great screech. She flew towards Arthur but he shouted to her to stay back. He couldn't risk her landing in the quicksand.

Thinking it couldn't get worse, a swathe of movement caught his eye on the dune top – a group of figures on horseback appeared. Arthur knew the crew's fate was sealed. It was all going to end in disaster and they'd barely reached halfway.

Arthur was now sunk up to his chest. The more he fought it, the more it pulled him in. He closed his eyes as the sound of horse's hooves thumping against the sand surrounded him.

CHAPTER 16

CITADEL KINGS

More figures on horseback galloped down the sand dune. But instead of cries of distress from the crew, there were cheers.

Arthur opened his eyes to see a grey-bearded man, wearing a bell-shaped hat with a band of thick fur around the rim, staring down at him.

"Be calm," the man said in Lontonian. "The way out is to pull your legs to the surface. Don't fight it. Control your breathing, try to manoeuvre your chest forward."

The man's voice was calming, and as Arthur followed what he was told, his legs eased upward.

"That's it, keep going."

As Arthur pushed his chest down, his legs rose, then a little more, until they were almost free.

"Now try to monkey-crawl your way a little, then we can pull you out."

Soon, arms grabbed him and he was back on firm ground, although the gloopy mixture clung to his clothes and his boots felt heavy as lead.

Maudie rushed over. "Arty, what the clanking cogs happened to you?"

"I fell." He glared at the bandit from the quicksand who was being tied up.

"King Temur! Your timing is impeccable!" Harriet called as she approached.

The man who had helped Arthur gave a nod. Arthur's eyes widened – he'd been saved by a king! He was mesmerized by the elaborate gold embroidery of King Temur's rich red robes.

Another man, dressed similarly, jumped from his horse.

"King Batzorig!" Harriet said. She clasped his hands and kissed him on both cheeks.

"I've told you a hundred times, just call me Batzorig!" His smile was the warmest Arthur had seen, snuggled inside his grey pointed beard.

Arthur and Maudie had never met a king, let alone two together. They stood there, not knowing whether to bow.

"Temur is still so serious, I see," Harriet said to Batzorig, loud enough for the other king to hear, but with a grin on her face.

Temur kissed her on each cheek. "One of us must take our kingly duties seriously, or nothing would get done and the Citadel would be chaos."

Batzorig laughed. "Done? Why must something always be done?"

"Because rogues like this are always ready to cause imbalance." Temur directed his men in tying up and searching the remaining bandits, while the crew of the *Aurora* were checked by Dr Quirke for any injuries.

"Did they steal from you, Harriet?" Batzorig asked.

"No, but I think they were after the sky-ship."

"So, this is the fine ship you've been planning for so long?" Temur said, raising his eyebrows and giving a nod and smile of approval. "She is . . . unusual looking, but she has a definite charm and interest to her shape." One of Temur's men handed him a pouch. "What's this? Enough silver to feed a village for a year. They seem remarkably rich for bandits, and I believe they are your First Continent coins." He passed one to Harriet.

Harriet examined them. "Yes, they are. How strange."

"Perhaps someone did not want you to proceed. Maybe their intention was personal?" said Batzorig.

Arthur looked to Maudie – could it be one of the other ships?

"Come to the Citadel. You will be quite safe there – we will question these crooks," said Temur.

Harriet nodded. "Thank you. We were on our way there, of course."

"Now we will see which is faster: your fine ship, the. . .?"

"The *Aurora*," Harriet said proudly.

"The *Aurora*, or my beautiful Altan." Batzorig laughed and mounted the horse beside him. Its coat was shiny as sweet chestnuts and its mane plaited with gold thread. It observed them with intelligent eyes. Batzorig whispered close to its ear and the horse neighed approvingly.

Definitely sapient, Arthur thought.

*

After washing Arthur in what little water they could spare, Maudie insisted on cleaning and polishing his arm to a high sheen while the crew of the *Aurora* took off again, chasing King Batzorig and King Temur, who galloped across the diminishing sand dunes, to where green patches gave way to crop fields and then a strange rocky formation rising above the plains. As they drew closer, Arthur saw it was a great city built on the rock. It was magnificent – as though its monumental structures of engraved walls, elegant rooftops and ornate columns had grown from the stone.

As the *Aurora* descended, people rushed along the jetty. Harriet threw a rope towards them, and soon the ship was anchored, and the gangplank lowered. The crew were greeted by crowds dressed in long robes and frocks of crimson red, sunrise gold, sapphire blue and the green of spring grass. Most people wore hats or headdresses that were heavily embroidered or trimmed with dangling beads.

A smiling and pink-cheeked child ran towards

Arthur, bearing a bright green scarf made of a shiny material. She looped it around his neck and said something in the language Arthur did not understand, then giggled.

Batzorig and Temur greeted them.

"I do believe the power of four legs is still better than these machines!" Batzorig laughed, although Arthur knew that Harriet had been going slower than she could have.

"And you've developed the water technology since we last met? There wasn't a trace of smoke in the air as you flew – most remarkable and, as pitch wasn't on the advance supply list, we hoped it would be true," said Temur.

"No need for pitch and she flies like a dream. She's built from within my home – it was the best way to keep it secret."

"The perfect cover from prying eyes!" Batzorig clapped his hands excitedly.

"Indeed. If we could trouble you to refill our water while we're here?"

"Of course, the wells of the Citadel are never dry." Batzorig gestured to an elaborate fountain sparkling in the sun.

Then they led the crew to a great stone hall carpeted by colourful rugs, with silver platters filled with exotic-looking fruits, colourful dishes of grain and vegetables, plump dumplings and rich sauces.

The crew sat on the rugs and scooped the food into small dishes and ate with their hands.

"So, your competitors didn't know your ship existed?" said Temur to Harriet.

"No, and a good job too. Other explorer families showed a great interest in the race to South Polaris. But each one dropped out as time went on, suddenly coming into more wealth or facing mysterious problems with their ships."

"Bought off or sabotaged?" said Batzorig.

Harriet shrugged. "Who can say?"

"Can we not persuade you to forget this challenge and stay here? We have everything you could ever want: fine food, fresh springs, the best company – what is the point of always exploring anyway?" said Batzorig.

"Indeed, it is a mystery to me," said Temur. "Besides, there are reasons people do not live in Moz Gazar: a sea that would swallow you for breakfast."

Batzorig continued, "Storms that could eat you

for dinner, biting cold, fearsome bodul chona – you must be out of your minds!" He laughed.

"Moz Gazar is what they call the Third Continent," Harriet said, seeing Arthur's confused expression. "The names we use are rather arrogant, putting ourselves first and letting everything else we discover in the Wide fall in behind us."

"And what's bodul chona?" Arthur asked.

Batzorig narrowed his eyes. "Legend says one of the largest creatures in the Wide lives in the great frozen forests of Moz Gazar – enormous creatures as cunning as humans. You would call them. . ." He looked to Temur for translation.

"Great wolves."

Arthur's stomach clenched.

Temur shook his head and affectionately put a hand on Batzorig's arm. "Hush, this talk is scaring them, Batzorig. Anyway, we need not travel to the ends of the earth to see the deadliest creatures in the world – they are all around us."

"Very true," Harriet said.

"It's all right, Harrie – we've met enough of you mad explorers to know there's no talking you out of going," said Batzorig.

"Thank you. We do appreciate your kind offer, but we must fly on into the night if we are to keep on schedule."

"Well, everything is prepared for you," said Temur. He clapped his hands and servants were soon trooping through the room bearing bundles and baskets on their heads and in their arms: plush furs, exotic spices and powders, dried, leathery meats and sweet, shrivelled fruits. "Load the supplies on to the sky-ship," he ordered.

Felicity wiggled her great feet from side to side, saying, "Bless my soul," repeatedly. "The things we shall cook, Arthur Brightstorm!"

"Brightstorm, you say?" Temur enquired fiercely.

Arthur froze. Had they heard what the Lontown papers had reported, even in this distant land?

Felicity put a protective arm around him and Maudie.

"Yes, these are Ernest Brightstorm's children," Harriet said, indicating Maudie too.

Temur's frown melted into a warm smile and both he and Batzorig laughed.

"And siblings of the sun and moon, I see more

clearly, now you are not covered in sand," Batzorig noted.

"He means twins," Harriet said.

"I call sun!" Maudie said, looking across and smiling widely at Arthur.

"You met our father?" Arthur said.

"Indeed, we last saw him on the way south many moon-cycles ago, and once before as a younger man. What a force of warmth and kindness he was, a fine example of the best of the First Continent," Temur said.

"We were sorry to hear of his passing." Batzorig put his hand to Maudie's cheek. "May I?"

"Don't be afraid; he likes to think he can see the inner person – it's our Second Continent mysticism, you might say. Pay no mind to it," said Temur.

"Yet he is remarkably accurate," Harriet nodded.

Maudie smiled and Batzorig shut his eyes.

"Ah, so much knowledge," he gave an excited giggle, "and a great creator too. Oh yes, I see you will go far and push boundaries of technological discovery." He opened his eyes. "Such a brain! You are welcome in our Citadel any time."

He shuffled towards Arthur, who wasn't sure he

wanted everything he felt inside to be exposed.

Seeing him flinch back, Temur smiled at Arthur. "The boy doesn't want it, Batzorig," he said softly.

But Batzorig waved him away and put a warm hand to Arthur's cheek.

"Ah, wild like a bird on the wing… but sad…" He was quiet for an uncomfortably long time. "Hmm, strange, I cannot quite see you yet. But perhaps you must see yourself first, before anyone else can."

Arthur felt deflated.

"Ignore his peculiar ways," Temur said. "We all walk our own road. Now, are you certain we cannot tempt you to refresh in the kingly quarters, a soft bed for the night?"

Harriet smiled. "We appreciate the offer, but time is against us. This is a race to South Polaris and even a few more chimes may count against us. Did the *Victorious* pass this way?"

"Indeed, not two days ago. And another ship, the *Fire-Bird*, was not far behind. They bought quantities of food but will have to stop off in the southern mines for their pitch. We have all but eradicated pitch from the city with the new water systems in place," Temur said proudly.

"They'll pay a hefty sum from those crooks," said Batzorig.

"Good, that refuelling stop will gain us time," Harriet said. "Now let me settle our great debt to you for these wonderful supplies."

Both Batzorig and Temur raised their hands. "No, no, we will not hear of it, with all that your good parents did for us during the siege of Gamutte. Their gravity irrigation system saved our lives!"

"No, really," Harriet tried, but Temur would not let her protest.

"Think nothing of it, dear friends," he said.

Harriet smiled. "Well, I have more books for you." Seeing Arthur and Maudie's panicked expressions, she added to them, "Don't worry, these have been in crates – they're not from the ship's library. Welby, if you could show Batzorig's good people where to find them."

Batzorig clapped his hands together. "How exciting – books are the greatest gift."

A guard approached Temur and spoke in his ear. Temur turned to Harriet. "The bandits are giving nothing away. We don't have more answers for you at this time, I'm afraid."

Harriet nodded, then said her goodbyes.

"Be careful, and make sure you win, for your good crew, and for Ernest Brightstorm." Temur made a whirling gesture to the sky and closed his eyes in a moment of thought.

Arthur and Maudie turned to leave the hall, but Batzorig stopped them.

"Before you go, you must tell me of your silver arm, Arthur."

Maudie jumped in. "The original arm was eaten by a huge crocodile in the Spice Islands in the west – you should've seen what he did to the crocodile." She gave a knowing nod.

Batzorig laughed heartily. "I meant, who made this wonderful construction?"

Maudie's freckles blushed brightly on her cheeks. "Oh, it was me."

Batzorig nodded, clearly impressed. "Why, of course you did. See, I am never wrong, Temur." He put an arm around Temur and hugged him close. "She could teach the Citadel ironmongers and engineers a thing or two, don't you think? And so well maintained; why, the metal shines like a mirror!"

Maudie smiled proudly.

"If you ever need work, we would welcome you here. Our universitas may not be as grand as Lontown, but in engineering and mathematics you will find no finer teachers," said Temur.

"Did you hear that?" Maudie looked at Arthur.

He nodded and smiled at her – there was that Maudie-shaped hole in the world again, waiting to be filled by his sister. But his wasn't there – he only had the hole inside of him, the void of not knowing what happened to Dad, of not knowing where he fitted in the world any more. And the way Batzorig had looked at him earlier hadn't helped with his doubt.

The crew made their way back to the *Aurora*, each to their own position on the ship.

A voice suddenly called out, "Wait, there's still a load of lemons!"

"Fresh lemons?" Felicity called, her eyes wide.

Someone dashed up the gangplank with a great basket of lemons and handed them to Felicity. Arthur breathed in the scent. Dad used to make the best lemon iced biscuits whenever they had the fruits in Lontown market, but they were rare in the First Continent.

"Twice the size of any lemons I've ever seen! They've positively made my toes tingle! Thank you, King Batzorig!" Felicity called.

Suddenly, a thought flashed through Arthur's mind about Ermitage Wrigglesworth's book.

"What is it?" Maudie asked. "You've got that look where I can see the cogs of your brain turning."

"There's something I need to check in the library. Meet me there after duties," he said.

The crew of the *Aurora* waved goodbye, then hurried to their positions, ready for take-off.

Nobody noticed the large silver insect scuttle along the bow, take flight and speed away.

CHAPTER 17

THE LAST POST

That evening after leaving the Citadel, Arthur hurried from his duties to the library. He found Ermitage Wrigglesworth's book and turned to the section on explorer families.

Maudie rushed in. "Sorry, Meriwether needed me to fix her weather glass."

"I've only just got here. Felicity wanted to try some of the new spices we got from the Citadel – she's calling them Citadel cookies, and she's now working on a new recipe, Batzorig buns!"

"Oh, that sounds wrong!"

Arthur flicked through the journal until he reached *Vane*.

"So, what's your revelation?"

Arthur examined the family's meticulously drawn explorer symbol.

He saw instantly what had been bothering him about the drawing. Something he was certain wasn't meant to be there – the tiniest lemon had been drawn in the centre of the rose. He smiled.

"Look at that!"

"What?"

"Well, you saw Madame Vane's tattoo when she visited us at Beggins Hall. I'm pretty sure there wasn't a lemon in the middle of the rose!"

Maudie laughed. "Why would anyone do that?"

The natural light was fading. Arthur lit a candle and moved it close to the page. That's when he saw the strange marks shining in the candlelight, in the spaces between the lines. He held the candle nearer. "Curious," he mumbled and moved his eye-line flat to the page. The mysterious markings were letters – hidden writing, not clear enough to read. "Of course!" he suddenly cried. "Wait here, Maudie. I need to pop to the kitchen."

Soon Arthur arrived back with lemon juice in a cup and Felicity's pastry brush. He dipped the brush, wiped a little on the side of the cup, then ran it over the paper wherever he could see the glint of hidden letters. Slowly words appeared. Beside the characteristics, it now said:

Ambitious
Shrewd
Ruthless

His heart thumped as more words revealed between the lines.

This rare dye is collected from the accumulation of crushed shells (note: the creatures must be alive when crushed in order to secrete the deepest of colour – only produced when the beetle is in a state of distress). The cruellest of exploits.

A cold shiver ran through him – the thought of crushing living creatures to colour fabric was horrible. The seemingly innocent passage about how the

Vanes had traded with the Spice Islands and formed relationships with them now informed that they'd used excessive force to take from the indigenous people. The Vanes had even made some of them leave their homes to become servants and had stolen children from their families, setting them to work in pitch mines. The hidden truth revealed that the real Vanes explored by stealing and forcing their authority wherever they went.

"But Eudora seems so..."

"Nice," Arthur finished.

Maudie shook her head. "What a horrible heritage."

"I wonder if she knows about her family's terrible past."

"What if she does know, and..."

"What if she's like her ancestors?"

"That means she might be..." Maudie looked horrified.

"The one behind our kidnapping."

"Think about it."

"The offer of a new life."

"Then, when that didn't work..."

"She really didn't want us to go."

"Then the bandits were paid by someone."

"She's trying to stop us from looking."

"Or finding something."

Their eyes met.

*

The *Aurora* flew relentlessly. There wasn't much time to enjoy the Second Continent flashing by beneath them, as the reality of keeping up the checks and routine of daily life while trying to keep on schedule meant not much time for fun.

At nightfall, a week after leaving the Citadel, there was still no sign of the *Victorious*. The temperature continued to drop rapidly the further south they flew, and any sign of people completely faded away. They were at the most southern point of the Second Continent, where they needed to land and replenish the water supply. Harriet was looking for the place on the map called the Last Post. Arthur remembered the name from the day at the Geographical Society. It was where the fuel had supposedly been stolen from the *Victorious*. Below, there came into view a huddle of buildings glowing orange in firelight, the only sign of life in the vast, star-speckled, moonless bay.

They landed and were greeted by a friendly young woman called Solongo. She was so pleased to see them, Arthur thought it must have been ages since she'd seen another person. Harriet said she'd met her once before when she'd travelled this far south a few years ago. After embracing every member of the crew, Solongo made them a fishy soup in a big pot on the bonfire. The sea lay motionless and the sky cloudless. The dark was so thick at the edges it was as though the rest of the world had been erased and all that existed was the small cluster of huts on the shoreline, and the crew of the *Aurora* grouped around the blaze, faces bathed in warm cinnamon light.

The sound of the sea tickling the beach disappeared beneath the deep baritone of Welby's song and the jolly twang of strings. Welby was so different the further away from Lontown they were, more relaxed. The crew sat on great rocks which looked as though they had been placed there by giant hands in a forgotten time. Solongo fluttered around the group like an excited butterfly, filling their glasses with her akhi hut brew, while heads bobbed and feet tapped to Welby's banjo, his white-haired head bouncing with the rhythm of the song.

My name is Welby Wild-o, my hut's in
Solongo's bay
Here she makes her akhi brew that'll take
your breath away
The walls have holes and the roofs are shot,
The rafters blow and the floorboards rot,
But nevertheless, you must confess, and hear
this from my mouth,
It's the most palatial dwelling you will find
this far south.

Arthur watched from a short distance; he put his hand to the locket which he kept around his neck, hidden beneath his shirt. The hull of the *Aurora* felt warm against his back – even though the engines weren't running, she watched over the group, keeping them safe. He could almost feel her breathing with him as though she was a living being.

Maudie glanced over, frowned curiously and beckoned him. She mouthed *Are you all right?*

He smiled and nodded, but tonight he felt on the outside.

Solongo bounded over to him with her akhi. "Come drink, warm for your long journey."

He shook his head. "I'm fine, thank you."

She smiled and began walking back to the group.

"Solongo."

The young woman turned back.

"Were you here when the last expedition passed?"

"Always here, ten years."

"Did you see anything when the last expedition was here? The two sky-ships?"

"What you mean?" She frowned.

"One of the ships, the *Victorious*, her fuel was stolen in the night. Did you see anyone take it? Did you hear anything?"

Solongo paused for a while as though working out his words, then shook her head. "Sorry. Solongo sleep, always long! When I wake, all ships gone." She shrugged and laughed, then returned to the group.

Behind the disintegrating huts of the shingle shore, white stones stood sentry in a picket-fenced enclosure. Arthur stood and wandered over, drawn to them, and carefully opened the gate. He ran his hand over one of the stones and felt the indent of symbols.

"They're gravestones."

Arthur jumped. He turned to see a figure behind him, wild hair tipped orange with the soft glow from her torch flame.

"I'm sorry, I didn't mean to scare you. I was seeking a moment of calm," Harriet said. The gate creaked shut and her feet crunched across the scattered pebbles.

"Why do all the stones face south?" he asked.

"They face their last journey. Some were whalers, others explorers. Before the sky-ships, attempts were made in sea-ships but none survived – the waters close to the Third Continent are too unpredictable, with terrible fierce waves and areas filled with icebergs."

"Not quite the Silent Sea, then?"

"It was named not for the movement of the waves, but the silence of death for those who dare attempt a crossing," she said.

He rested his hand on one of the stones.

"Solongo was here the night the *Victorious* and *Violetta* were. She didn't hear a thing."

"Ah, the fuel theft."

"He wouldn't have done it."

"I knew your father from universitas. He gave the occasional lecture on geology. Fascinating, they were. He was a kind professor, and he knew his subject inside out. He seemed a true and honest man."

"So, you don't believe it?"

"People sometimes do things out of character when driven by high stakes."

His heart sank.

She put her hand on his shoulder. "But my instinct tells me he didn't."

Arthur smiled.

"The brief time our paths crossed you must've been very young, but I do recall him mentioning his children. When you came to Four, Archangel Street I recognized something in you. At first I couldn't place it. Then I realized there was something in the slant of your eyebrows, the freckles, the windswept hair, that determined stare. You look so like him, less the beard, of course!"

A cheer came from around the campfire as Welby finished another song. Arthur looked up at the clear sky speckled with stars. The night breeze carried an ice chill ashore.

"I think Eudora Vane had something to do with what happened," he said.

"It was certainly no accident that someone didn't want you to come looking for answers, and after the incident before the Citadel it has certainly been on my mind. But what makes you suspect Madame Vane?"

"Do you know Ermitage Wrigglesworth's book in the library?"

"Ah, his handwritten journal that preceded the book. My great-aunt was good friends with Wrigglesworth. It's one of my favourites."

"I found hidden writing between the lines. It tells the truth about the awful things the Vanes have done, things that have been kept secret from Lontown."

"Hidden writing?"

"It's revealed with lemon juice. There was a clue in the drawing."

"I'm impressed, Arthur Brightstorm. I had no idea!"

He told her what he'd read in the secret writing.

She nodded thoughtfully. "The Vanes are an explorer family who go back a long way. They're notoriously secretive. One hears whispered rumours, but they are quickly brushed away. The Vanes have sovereigns and a powerful name. If they want things hidden, I imagine there is always someone to bribe."

"Just after we received your letter, at Beggins Hall—"

"Yes, I was surprised that my note was not delivered successfully to Brightstorm House. It wasn't easy working out how to find you."

"The Begginses are the horrible people we were sent to live with in the Slumps after we found out about Dad. Our guardian, Mistress Poacher, sold us to the Begginses. They treated us as their servants. You see, the insurer told us there was some clause in Dad's insurance and we lost everything."

"How terrible for you. I'm so sorry, Arthur."

"Well, after we received your letter, we were visited by Madame Vane. She offered us a chance to live comfortably. She also tried to dissuade us from joining this crew by telling us you didn't have a worthy sky-ship."

Harriet's eyes narrowed. "Curious behaviour, indeed. But we must be careful of accusing without hard facts. What you have found out sets off alarm bells about Madame Vane, but I'm afraid it's not enough." She paused. "Even so, best we keep our distance from their ship where possible."

Arthur nodded.

They stood in silence for a while before Harriet said, "This is the last post south of the world we know. Beyond this point there are no people, no traders; we enter the frozen Third Continent. The journey ahead will be tough. Are you ready for that, Arthur? If you have any doubt, now is the time to say."

"I'm ready, Harriet," he promised.

"You are a solver of problems, Arthur. I see it every day – you find a way. We *will* get to South Polaris, we will finish what your father couldn't, and you will restore honour to your name."

Her assurance was contagious. It reminded him of Dad – he'd always made him feel confident.

"I'm so glad you and Maudie made it to the ship.

Thirteen is a very unlucky crew number, and we're going to need lots of luck in the coming moon-cycle!" She held the gate open for him. "Come on, let's stop Solongo drowning the crew in her akhi or they'll not be fit to fly."

CHAPTER 18

GREAT GLACIES

Later they waved a sad goodbye to Solongo and took off across the Silent Sea towards the Third Continent.

Harriet looked ahead, a huge smile illuminating her face. "As of this moment, I'm somewhere I've never been before." She turned to Arthur beside her. "Thrilling, isn't it?"

Arthur knew how she felt. He was leaving the human world behind, going where Dad had stepped into the unknown. It was the closest he'd felt to his father since he'd left for the expedition.

Harriet estimated ten days to cross the Silent

Sea. By the third day the sea was moody, with waves as high as the *Lontown Chronicle* Tower. Arthur couldn't believe anyone had attempted to sail to the Third Continent on a sea-bound ship. The crew carried on through the relentless wind and driving rain, doing their best to keep dry below deck whenever they could, but mostly it was all hands on deck to keep the ship from being blown off course.

Arthur was on bailing duty, sweeping the build-up of water towards the drains. It wasn't the easiest task for him, as relentless, one-handed sweeping soon made his arm ache, so he'd managed to clamp his iron arm around the broom, which worked better.

There was a rare break in the wind, although the rain was unforgiving. He caught sight of a dark shape coming towards them. He paused.

"Ahoy there!" Harriet called.

There was an inaudible call back.

Arthur rushed to the bow. It was the *Fire-Bird*. One balloon was deflated and her mast was bent.

The stricken vessel steered close to the *Aurora*, where they could see a man holding a brass megaphone. He shouted, "We're heading back – our mast has fractured, and we've already used half our fuel fighting the wind! Turn back, if you know what's good for you and the crew!"

"A wise choice by the look of your ship, Captain!" Harriet shouted back as they chugged past. "Thank you for your concern, but we're still a stout ship and crew; there's plenty of life in us yet! Travel safe!"

"Only the *Victorious* between us and South Polaris, then," Welby said, with a broad smile.

They carried on, day after day, battling vicious winds – some days going full steam ahead just to stay still.

On the twelfth day, the weather had calmed and Felicity was taking a break from preparing dinner because her feet ached so terribly she had to get her weight off them for the afternoon. She'd left Arthur in charge of preparing her special galley stew, which they ate every five days, so he knew how to prepare it with his eyes shut. He was chopping potatoes on his spike board when he heard the rumble of feet on wooden floorboards directly above him.

Arthur was desperate to run and see what was going on, but the galley couldn't be left unattended if the stove was lit. As Felicity reminded him often, fire and wooden flying ships don't mix unless you want a quick descent. Shutting down the valves and starving the fire of oxygen took time. He impatiently tapped his iron arm until the flame went out, before dashing out of the door along the corridor and up the stairs to the deck. When he reached above, the crew were all staring over the side of the ship, pointing.

The *Aurora* had descended to a short distance above the now calm waves. Blocks of ice as tall as the great buildings of Uptown Lontown dotted across the sea, luminous blue in the late afternoon light. All of a sudden, something great and dark rose from the water between two icebergs, and a huge chuff of water sprayed into the air. The creature arched its huge body slowly then submerged again.

Maudie jumped beside him tugging his arm. "Arty, look! Aren't they amazing?"

Then a group of four rose together – two large and two smaller. He had never seen such enormous creatures. The scene was breathtaking.

"It's a family," he said.

Two wrinkled hands grasped the edge of the ship beside Arthur. "They're called great glacies and they're whales – the largest creature in the world." Welby's white hair had become longer and less perfect throughout the journey. He even had a bit of a beard growing, which Arthur thought suited him – he looked like an original explorer from the illustrations in *Exploring in the Second Age*. "They were almost hunted out of existence."

"By the people of the Second Continent?" Arthur asked. They seemed so in touch with nature and animals there, he couldn't imagine it.

"No – by the First. The great glacies weren't always this far south. They were common in the Culldam Sea and further north, but the body of a glacie fetched a high price in Lontown. Great animals were slaughtered just so some Uptowner could show off a whale-skin clutch at a dinner party or someone like Eudora Vane could have luminous skin with the fine oils derived from the blubber."

"So they stay here where the rough seas keep them safe?"

"As much as they can, but they need to travel to warmer waters to feed when it's the harshest winter."

"The whales should hunt the humans and see how they like it," Maudie said.

"Indeed!" Welby laughed. It was lovely to see his serious mask drop for a moment, before he resumed his orderly tone. "Now, back to work, there's much to do – this isn't a tea party, you know, no matter what Miss Wiggety says."

Harriet approached Welby, holding the temperature reader attached to her belt. "It's dropped several degrees in the past chime, and at night it will plunge, which means we're nearly at the Third Continent. Miss Wiggety, I want you to go straight to the stores and hand out the warm clothes we picked up in the Citadel. The cold will sink its chill teeth straight into our bones if we stay in these any longer." She called to the crew to form a queue in the galley corridor and get their new clothes, while Arthur rushed down to relight the stove.

Five minutes later, Arthur hurriedly slopped extra-large portions of stew into overfilling bowls and handed them to the crew, who ate quickly before leaving to dress in their new kit.

As Arthur was clearing up, Harriet arrived back. "I've brought your new clothes." She put the huge pile of fur and oilskin on the table.

Arthur carried the bundle back to his cabin

to change. Putting on the furs and oilskins was awkward, and he wished he had Maudie there to help. The buttons were in unfamiliar places and stiff, so were tricky to do one-handed, let alone getting the smock jacket over his iron arm. He knew it would be far simpler to take the arm off, but he wanted to make sure he could still wear it as it was bound to be useful as they continued in the Third Continent. It was too awkward to force his iron arm through, so he pushed his feet into the fur boots, and went back to the galley. He secured the jacket into his chopping clamp and sliced through the material of the arm with Felicity's sharpest knife. His iron arm eased through the sleeve hole, fitting snugly. By the time he'd finished, his cheeks were bright crimson with the effort, so he hurried to the deck where the cold slap of wind was a welcome relief. The last sliver of sunlight evaporated as the clouds above met.

"It's dropped five degrees in ten minutes," Maudie said, shivering in the dark.

Snow drifted from above. Soft and light, it fluttered down, icing the ship and the crew.

"We need everyone scraping – if the ice forms

on the ship and the wings it'll weigh us down too much," Welby called out.

By evening, the temperature had dropped again, and Harriet ordered a shift pattern for clearing the snow through the night and sent everyone else below deck to get some sleep, while she and Welby took turns navigating the ship and sleeping. Even inside, the *Aurora* seemed to be frosting over and the woodwork creaked and strained. Parthena and Queenie had formed a truce and were below deck, snuggled together, keeping warm with everyone else.

Keen to see the snow again, Arthur volunteered for the early shift and woke at dawn. He could only remember it snowing a few times in Lontown and nothing on this scale. He found a metal flask and made tea to take to Harriet on the deck.

At the hatch, the ice wind took his breath away. Arthur peered through and watched Harriet at the wheel steering the *Aurora* onwards. Her silhouette was utterly still, strong, as if nothing could knock her from her position, her mop of unstyled hair danced in the wind and her gaze was fixed ahead.

He crossed the deck and passed her the flask.

"Thank you. The snow's eased – look." She pointed to the horizon.

Ahead, an endless white carpet spread across the landscape, broken by thousands of ice-topped hills stretching from east to west and glimpses of greenery. Harriet passed him the binoscope. "It's quite something, isn't it?"

The stretch of white was crisp and fresh, every edge sharp and defined. Arthur took a large breath and crystal cold filled his lungs. The sea below was speckled with thousands of ice chunks lapping into the frozen shore. In the far distance the undulations petered out. "Is that the Everlasting Forest?"

"Yes, I believe so, but we won't reach that for some time. We'll set down on the coast in the bay, change the water and check everything is in order before we embark on crossing further. Porridge for breakfast, and let's break open a jar of Batzorig's best honey."

He rushed below and helped Felicity as the crew woke and began their duties. Seeing how eager he was to see more of the Third Continent, Felicity said she would take care of breakfast and make sweet honeyed tea to combat the cold. She let him off his duties to return to the deck. Parthena flew on to his iron arm, and butted her head to his cheek. "I agree, Parthena," said Arthur, "it's amazing here." Then she took flight into the clear morning sky. Arthur watched her through the binoscope, her great white wings elegantly working with the undulations of the wind.

They had descended and were coming in to land in the bay when Parthena circled the ship and made a succession of screeches. "What the grinding grommets has got into her?" he said.

There was the rumble of engines as the *Victorious* took flight from the shore of the Third Continent.

Harriet took the binoscope and looked through. "It's all right, Arthur. We predicted we'd catch them up around here. It's a little sooner than expected, but that's a good thing. We'll land, change the water supply and then take straight off again. Their engines will be on half power to conserve fuel, so this is where we gain an advantage." She passed Arthur the binoscope.

As he looked through he saw a flash of silver – he

chased it with his gaze. It was a strange flying silver insect. "Look!" He pointed. "What's that doing all the way out here?"

But when he passed the binoscope back to Harriet, it had gone.

"Maybe it was just a reflection on the glass," she said.

But he was certain it wasn't.

CHAPTER 19

THE CASE AGAINST EUDORA VANE

The *Aurora* landed on the icy shore of the Third Continent. Arthur couldn't believe he'd travelled across so far. He felt he'd stepped into a wintery dream. While Harriet, Maudie and some other members of the crew busied themselves with the water change and their equipment checks, Arthur and Felicity walked a little way up the coastline in case there was anything that could be added to the stores, but it was rock and ice as far as they could see. There was an absolute quiet to the land, and if it hadn't been for the distant chug of the *Victorious*'s engines, Arthur would have felt as though they were the only living creatures in the entire Wide.

"We're here at last," Felicity said, smiling. "Is something bothering you, young Arthur?"

He shrugged. "I guess a small part of me thought that maybe my father had survived, but look at it here. Who could survive on their own?"

"Hope can drive us to do things we never thought possible, Arthur Brightstorm. Maybe you had to tell yourself that to give you the strength. And perhaps a part of the reason you came all this way wasn't just about your father."

He wasn't sure what she meant.

"You'll understand one day. Come on, there's clearly nothing edible around here!"

They soon took off again. Little by little, they were closing in on the *Victorious*. After half a day, as they were approaching the Everlasting Forest of the Third Continent, Harriet turned course south-westerly for a short time so that they could keep a safe distance from the rival sky-ship.

"We're nearly level with them!" Maudie called, looking through her uniscope.

The whole crew stood poised on the port-side deck, watching in anticipation.

As Harriet steered onwards, Welby stood beside Maudie, looking through the binoscope and checking his readings.

After a moment he declared, "The *Aurora* is ahead!"

The crew cheered, but Arthur remained quiet, focusing on the forest below.

Maudie approached him. "What's the matter, Arty? You should be pleased."

"I am, it's just. . ."

The trees were packed tightly together; it was impossible to see what lurked below. All Arthur could think about were the great prints that the Vane crew had found by the Brightstorm ship and the huge pelt the Vane crew had brought back. He stared at the frozen treetops passing silently below.

"If you wanted to hide a secret, it would be in there," he said.

But Maudie had already left and was talking with Welby and exchanging notes.

They flew on into the night, which was only short now they were so far south, lasting just a few chimes. The skies were eerily clear and the almost full moon illuminated a vast landscape of white trees. It was beautiful, yet there was something unnerving about it – a looming blackness that seemed to be watching them. The further they went, the more he could feel it in his head – strange words and thoughts, almost as though the darkness was talking to him. But that sounded ridiculous.

A hand on his arm made him jump.

"Are you all right? You've gone pale as the moon," Maudie said, passing him a steaming cup.

"It's the forest – it's so . . . black."

She frowned. "It looks pretty bright with all the snow."

"No, I mean inside the forest. I can hear something."

Maudie frowned. "You're thinking of the beasts, aren't you?"

He nodded.

"Arty, you need sleep. We can't land until light, and we'll be perfectly safe all together."

"Hm," he said, peering down. Were the whispers trying to tell him the sinister truth?

"Arty, are you sure you're all right?" She pulled

his arm. "Come on, you're going to our cabin for a rest."

*

Arthur fell asleep quickly. The next thing he knew, a great boom and shudder rumbled every cell in his body. He sat up, wide-eyed.

Maudie looked over the side of the bunk. "What the grinding grommets was that?" They both leapt out of bed and began pulling on their boots.

Footsteps thundered through the hallway. Suddenly the *Aurora* dipped at the front, sending them flying forward. They scrambled into the passageway.

Harriet dashed past. "There's been some sort of explosion in the engine. The pressure gauge is going through the roof. I'm shutting down the engine – she's going to blow again. Brace for a crash landing; wrap yourself in anything you can find. I'll guide her into the trees as best I can."

Arthur and Maudie ran back to their bunks, pulled the mattresses from their beds and wrapped them around themselves. The *Aurora* banked sideways and they lurched across the room. Through the portholes, the forest was a swathe of ghostly white-topped pines growing nearer by the second. The thought of going into the darkness of the forest was terrifying, but so was the thought of exploding mid-air.

"*Why do you come?*" He turned behind him to see who had spoken, but there was no one.

Arthur tumbled, then everything flew upward and hit the ceiling as the *Aurora* surged down. Flashes of white and darkness rolled past the window. Hideous crashing and splitting sounds were everywhere, and the hull juddered horribly. All he could see was the rush of branches as the sky-ship was engulfed by the forest.

With a horrible crack, splinters of wood flew through the air and again he tumbled. A bone-wrenching jolt threw him across the room – the cacophony of noise disappeared and everything went very still, silent and black.

*

Arthur groaned. Every part of his body ached. He wiggled his toes and fingers – yes, still there. He tried to open his eyes but his head pounded.

Someone wiped his forehead with a cloth, and he heard Dr Quirke's voice. "It's just a cut – you'll be all right. The crash probably knocked you out for a while but don't worry, everyone's alive. There are a few cracked ribs and nasty bruises – Welby has broken his wrist – but we were lucky."

Arthur sat up. His head thrummed and everything spun. He fought the urge to faint.

"Whoa, careful," Harriet said.

"I have to find Maudie," he said, trying to stand.

Harriet put a firm hand on him. "You need to be still. Maudie's fine; she's helping the wounded. I'll tell her you're awake."

The blurred shapes cleared – around was utter devastation. The *Aurora* had been torn apart and was in two halves. The surrounding trees were bent, snapped and charred, and debris littered the branches and forest floor. Parthena called from somewhere in the trees above.

"Stay here for a while – you took quite a bang to the head. I'll get a fire going."

As soon as Harriet had gone, he tried to get up again. Felicity ran over, her hair loose and dishevelled, and her apron torn. "Now, stay still – and that's an order," she said, waving her bent spoon at him.

"I guess the lucky spoon ran out of luck," he said.

She smiled and shook her head. "Oh, Arthur Brightstorm, joking at a time like this." Then she ripped up the edge from her apron and started rebandaging his head. "Let's sort this out. I was rushing the first time."

"What happened?"

"Some sort of explosion. It's a miracle we're all alive."

Maudie ran from behind the other half of the ship. "Thank goodness you're all right." She crouched beside him and helped Felicity tie his bandage.

They sat in sad silence and stared at the wreckage of the *Aurora*. A trail of smoke petered into the sky.

Arthur couldn't speak. They'd come so close.

After a while Harriet returned holding Arthur's iron arm. "I found this dangling in a tree. It scared the life out of me until I realized what it was. I've started a campfire, but we need to gather supplies and salvage what we can before the short night comes again." She sat beside Arthur, who stared into space. "Maudie, you can help Welby and Forbes assess the state of the engine and see what can be saved. I need to gather more wood for the fire or we'll freeze. Arthur, how's your head feeling now? Can you help?"

He nodded. He couldn't sit staring at the chaos and disappointment a moment longer.

"All right. I'll just tell the rest of the crew, then we'll go."

Arthur reached inside his iron arm. Thankfully the piece of paper from the book was still there. He unfolded it and read.

The Brightstorm moth, a new species discovered by Ernest Brightstorm in the Northern Isles, uses the light of the moon to ensure it travels in an absolutely straight line, allowing it to navigate successfully between two volcanic islands fifty miles apart, and never stray from its path.

He stared at the drawing of the Brightstorm moth, so intricate it looked real.

Maudie squeezed his shoulder. "Come on, I'll help you get your arm on before Harriet gets back."

*

The forest was silent apart from the frozen undergrowth crunching beneath their feet. Harriet led the way.

"We'll head back where the *Aurora* crashed through the trees and pick up some wood, and we may be able to find some evidence of what happened on the way."

Fractured trees and branches were all around, and the ground was littered with various bits of metal and wood from the ship.

"What will we do, Harriet?" Arthur said.

"We don't wallow. We try and find out what happened, we re-gather and make a new plan." Harriet pointed at one of the metal objects by Arthur's feet. "What's that?"

Arthur stooped and picked it up. It looked to be a piece of metal from the *Aurora*'s engine. Harriet examined it.

"It's from the hydra-valve. But these marks are very regular, almost as though it was gnawed through by. . ."

"By?" Arthur said.

"A creature."

"What are you saying?"

She stared at him, her eyes deadly serious. "It's ruptured. It would have likely caused a pump to blow. This looks like the explosion was deliberate."

Arthur raised his eyebrows. "The silver insect! I saw it when we reached the Third Continent shore. It was small enough to have slipped inside the ship's engine room unnoticed, but big enough to do some damage."

Harriet ran a hand through her wayward hair. "You think it could be a sapient creature, working on instruction?"

He paused; he couldn't believe he'd not made the connection. "Eudora Vane's brooch!"

"How hard was that knock to your head, Arthur?"

"You've seen the silver brooch she wears. Except I'm betting it's not jewellery at all, it's probably a sapient insect."

"You're saying it was sabotage?"

Arthur nodded. "And the other two ships had to drop out due to sudden damage; it's rather a coincidence, don't you think?"

Harriet nodded. "Let's gather the wood and get back. We need to tell the crew, in case you're right and Eudora tries anything else. We need to be wary of her whole team."

They fell silent as the forest darkened around them, and they gathered wood into a large pile. The trees seemed to squeeze in around them in the fading light.

Then he heard the voice in his head again. "*Why do you come?*" He flinched. It was probably the bang on the head messing with his mind.

Harriet stopped and looked at him. "Are you all right? Maybe we should go back."

He shook his head. "I'm fine."

"*Why do you come?*"

He looked through the trees. Dark shapes loomed in the gloom and he had the feeling they were being watched. "Did you hear that?"

"Hear what?"

He shook his head.

She paused and stared at him. "Come on – even in this light I can see how pale you've become. We've got enough wood for now. It's time to head back."

Arthur didn't argue. He locked his iron arm into an arc, which he used to hook a bundle of the firewood. They went back to the *Aurora*, Arthur glancing back over his shoulder every few moments.

Back at what remained of their ship, Felicity had gathered the scattered food supplies and organized them into rations. She was making soup in a big battered pot.

As the crew sat subdued around the fire, Harriet told them of Arthur's suspicions. Then a familiar rumbling sounded in the distance – the engines of the *Victorious*. They froze as it flew nearer, until it was almost on top of them. Harriet ordered everyone to the tree line. Arthur dashed behind a tree with Maudie, and Harriet behind one nearby.

From their hiding places, they watched as the ship appeared above them and came to a hovering standstill. Great gusts of smoke from the engines plumed into the devastated clearing made by the crash.

"Having a little problem, Miss Culpepper?" Eudora called.

Arthur looked from behind his tree, up through the clearing. Beside Eudora a man stood, holding a gun and grinning. It was Mr Smethwyck, the insurance representative who had visited them.

Maudie pulled him back. "Are you mad?"

"It's him, the man from the insurance – he's with her!"

"We'd offer to help, but time is short and we have the South Polaris to claim. If you could hand over your fuel, we could do with a little more," Eudora called.

"I'm afraid we don't have any pitch, Eudora," Harriet shouted.

Eudora laughed. "No pitch? Don't be absurd. What are you powered by?"

"All we need is water."

Arthur couldn't help but take another look. Eudora's expression was ice cold, her lips tight with fury. She muttered something, as though talking to herself, then the silver brooch unfurled its wings, and took flight in the direction of the sky-ship wreckage. It *was* a sapient insect.

It whizzed past Arthur, sharp mandibles gnashing. He thought of the marks in the damaged hydra-valve. The insect darted quickly amongst the wreckage of the *Aurora* looking for pitch, but of course there was none. It flew back to Eudora.

"Pitch or not, it seems your journey is over. Enjoy your time in the forest, Miss Culpepper – the short night will be here soon. When the native beasts tire of their meagre pickings, you'll be a veritable feast. If they don't get you, the elements soon will."

With that, the engines fired up and the *Victorious* headed onwards, leaving a great plume of pitch smoke choking through the trees.

"So much for the Explorers Code: 'Assist fellow travellers first.' Come on, let's get prepared for the night," Harriet said, shaking her head.

Arthur pulled Maudie to the side. "I can't sit here while she gets away with what she did. Come on, Maudie, we're going after them. We can sneak away while no one's looking."

"Arty, you're not thinking straight."

"We'll lose them unless we go now!"

Maudie rolled her eyes. "We need to think – you can't just go running off into the forest alone."

But there was no time. The *Victorious* was disappearing, and Arthur hadn't come all this way for nothing. He was going to find Dad's ship – he'd chase the sound of the *Victorious* south until he found it. "Are you coming or not?"

She planted her feet and put her hands on her hips. "Arthur Brightstorm, you're not thinking."

"Fine!" he snapped.

Arthur stormed off into the forest.

Maudie shouted after him.

He broke into a run, trying desperately to keep up with the fading engines.

"Arthur, what are you doing?" Harriet called.

But he couldn't stop, because if he did, reality would catch up with him: that Dad was really gone for ever, that he had no idea what the future looked like any more, and that he might never find the truth and be able to clear the Brightstorm name. He charged onwards, the snow dragging at his feet and pine branches clawing at his clothes.

After a while, the hurried slur of footsteps through snow caught up with him. Harriet grabbed his shoulder. They both came to a standstill, gasping for breath. The *Victorious* was miles away already. It was hopeless.

Harriet glared at Arthur. "What in all the Wide are you thinking? I have responsibility for the crew, Arthur Brightstorm, and I will do everything I can to protect their lives, and that includes you. I have a duty to keep you safe in the most trying of environments, and you're not helping me by running off!"

"Eudora Vane had something to do with what happened to Dad. I need to know." The tight lump in his throat stopped him saying any more. He swallowed back, trying not to burst into tears in front of Harriet.

She sat in the snow, leaning against a pine tree. "If you'd stayed still long enough to listen, I would have told you my plan."

"You have a plan?" He sat against the tree beside her.

Harriet smiled. "Always. I'm thinking we rest here for the short night, and at first light we head for the frozen lake with a core team of four. I need as many as I can to stay and salvage what's left of the *Aurora*. The front half of the ship looks viable, and the main balloon is intact. The blown pump is irreparable, but the other is relatively undamaged, so I'm instructing the crew to make a half ship out of the useable parts. Welby will be in charge here, directing the majority on repairs, while the core team will attempt to make it to South Polaris. When we return, the crew will have hopefully made a sky-ship able to get us at least back to Solongo at the Last Post."

He looked at the snowy forest floor, hoping beyond everything she meant he was going onwards with her. "We?"

"I want you to be part of the core team. I've seen your drive and resilience, and I know that I couldn't separate you from Maudie – as much as I think her engineering skills would be of use here with Welby, Forbes will be sufficient. We can't carry many supplies, so Felicity's food knowledge can keep us alive when things become more extreme. Gilly can take care of the food for the rest of the crew back here. We'll be on rations and it'll be colder than you've ever experienced, but I know you can do this, and I know how much clearing your family name means to you."

He could hardly speak. There was still hope.

Harriet continued. "Giving up isn't in my nature, or yours, it seems. But you *must* stop and think before acting, and you'll need to listen – not just to me, but to everyone. I can't have you taking off like that again." She raised her eyebrows.

"Sorry, it felt as though it was slipping away." But Arthur stopped suddenly, sure he glimpsed strange shapes through the trees and small circles of light reflected in the dark. He stared, squinting into the forest.

"What is it?" Harriet said.

The breath froze in his throat as he realized the lights were piercing green eyes staring right at them.

CHAPTER 20

THOUGHT-WOLVES

In Arthur's haste to chase the *Victorious*, he'd forgotten about the darkness within the forest.

"It's the beasts," he breathed.

Judging by the height of the eyes, the creatures were enormous: much taller than a person.

"Don't make any sudden movements," Harriet said. Emerald eyes shone in every direction. They were surrounded.

Then Arthur's head buzzed as though a wave of electricity passed through him, and he felt the creature in his thoughts, probing, testing, demanding. Inside his mind were powerful feelings that started to form words, like the messages he'd heard before, but it was too confusing. Harriet must have heard too this time, because they both clasped their ears to block it, but it was right inside of them.

"Run!" Harriet shouted, grabbing his arm.

But her sudden movement seemed to release the creatures, who charged from the surrounding forest, snow flying from beneath their great paws. Arthur and Harriet spun around frantically – but there was nowhere to go, and all he could see was fur and great white teeth coming for them.

An enormous beast, twice the height of him, pounced. It crashed into him and bowled him over, tumbling to the frozen earth, before pinning him with its great paws and huge muscular shoulders. Another held Harriet beside him.

Paralysed by fear, he shut his eyes tight, praying for it to be over quickly.

The creature's paws were heavy on his chest, the pinch of claws threatening to bite into him. The feeling was in his head again, forming into a word. It said *fear*, but it wasn't coming from him, it was coming from somewhere else. He tried to block it out and forced his eyes open.

The creature's lupine face stared down at him, its snout curled with a fierce snarl and its hackles raised. "*Do you fear?*" Its great shoulders tensed as it seemed to wait for his reply.

Arthur's whole body trembled, but he forced himself to stare back – Dad would have faced it head-on. If this was his end and it was to be the same as Dad, then he should at least try to be as brave as his father would have been. Terrible scenes raced through his head as he imagined these terrible creatures killing Dad and the crew.

The great wolf's head tilted, and then came the feeling inside his head again. Words trying to form. He didn't want it there.

"*Fear, you fear,*" the words said inside him. Perhaps his terror was sending him mad!

"Stop!" he blurted, shaking his head.

"Arthur, don't provoke it!" Harriet urged beside him.

"*Look,*" the voice in his head said. The claws dug into his chest.

"Just kill us and be done with it!" Arthur urged, and squeezed his eyes shut.

The voice sounded in his head strong and clear,

somehow calmer. "*Look.*" The pressure on Arthur's chest eased a little. He opened his eyes, his pulse racing in a constant stream of beats. The great beast's face was inches from his own, but for some reason it still held back from attacking.

More words rushed in Arthur's head – the creature was trying to communicate something. A question formed inside Arthur, something about hearing or listening. He forced himself to look into its eyes, and the words seemed clearer. "*Can you listen?*"

After a moment, Arthur nodded shakily. Words flashed through his mind too quickly to grasp, and he felt too panicked still to hear them. The sound of his own heart thumping against his ribs was louder than anything. "*Please don't hurt us,*" he thought.

The creature tilted its head again.

What did people say in situations like this, meeting strange hostile creatures? "*We come in peace,*" he thought, but it sounded ridiculous.

"*You are in pieces?*" came the reply in his head. The great wolf looked across to the one pinning Harriet. Arthur almost laughed despite the terror still gripping him. But the words were clearer this time, easier to comprehend, as though his brain was becoming used to these strange feelings and words. The wolf-like creature was talking to him through thought – and he couldn't believe it, but he could understand.

"*Peace, no harm,*" Arthur thought.

The wolf eased his paws from Arthur.

"*No harm,*" came the reply in Arthur's head.

"What's going on?" Harriet remained pinned beside him. "Welby said to bring guns as back-up, but I didn't listen – I said it was a slippery road, now I. . ." Her wolf growled.

"Harriet, I think we should just stay very still," Arthur said. "And try not to think anything aggressive."

Arthur slowly eased himself to sitting.

"*What are you?*" he thought.

The words were hard to understand but his brain turned it into something that sounded like "*Thought-wolves*". It seemed to describe them perfectly.

More words rushed him. "*Slower,*" he thought.

There was a pause, then the words came more slowly. "*We know you two-leg creatures.*"

He thought of Dad and swallowed.

"*Coming with your flying beasts, breathing smoke on to our snow forest.*" It growled and snarled at him. "*You came before and attacked us, killed one of my pack.*"

He looked across at Harriet who still looked terrified.

"*Please let us go. It wasn't us; we're not like that.*"

"*The sickly scent is in the air again.*"

Arthur understood what the wolf meant – Eudora. He remembered the pelt. "*We are peaceful. The ones who harmed your pack before – their leader was a female two-legs? The one with the sickly-sweet smell.*"

The wolf growled.

"*The one with a sickly scent told us you had killed a two-legs crew, a human pack.*"

"*We feed from the forest only.*"

Relief flooded through Arthur. The thought-wolves hadn't killed Dad or the crew – they had no reason to lie. "*We aren't your enemy. We're here looking for answers.*"

The thought-wolf paused in thought, then looked

at the one pinning Harriet. It released her. The others lost their aggression in an instant.

Arthur brushed himself down.

"What's going on? Can you hear strange buzzing?" Harriet said, her voice still panicked.

"I can hear it. They're communicating with us. But don't listen for words; listen for a feeling in their thoughts and they become words. It's how they speak with each other. And they didn't kill Dad and his crew – he said it was Eudora who attacked and killed one of their pack before."

Harriet stared at him, dumbstruck. "You've ... worked all that out with them? By thinking it?"

Arthur shrugged sheepishly.

"*I am Tuyok.*" The wolf bowed its head to him.

"*My name is Arthur.*" He gave a nod.

"*Your sky beast crashed?*"

"*Our ship? Yes, the female pack leader, she's called Eudora Vane. It was her fault. She doesn't lead our pack – she has a different ship, sky beast. She's flown onwards.*"

Tuyok paced around him. "*Why are you here?*"

"*We're racing to South Polaris – it's the furthest point south.*"

"To search for food?"

"No, we're going because, well, we've never been there. Humans, that is. Two-legs."

Tuyok looked curiously at him.

"And we're also here because my father and his crew died here, and we want to find out how."

"You seek truth?"

"Yes. And now we know they weren't killed by wolves, it's more important than ever that we find out what happened, and the answers are here somewhere, I'm certain."

Tuyok's thought presence left Arthur for a moment to speak with another thought-wolf.

"What's going on?" Harriet said, looking uncharacteristically pale.

"Are you all right? They don't mean us any harm."

Tuyok returned to him. *"We will take you where you must go, pack-leader Arthur."*

"Oh, I'm not pack-leader; she is," Arthur thought. He looked towards Harriet. "Did you hear? They're going to help us."

"I've still no idea what you're hearing. It's just a buzzing in my head that I can't make out."

"We can get you through the forest to the frozen lake where the ghost sky-ship lies, but that's as far as we travel."

"The ghost sky-ship?" he thought, realizing Tuyok meant Dad's ship, the *Violetta*. A small ripple of hope rushed through him.

"I am sorry, cub. The ghost sky-ship is a place of death and echoes. There have been no living two-legs in this land for many moon-cycles."

Arthur swallowed back the lump in his throat and grabbed the locket hanging around his neck. He'd been told before that his father was dead, but he had to keep on hoping, until he knew for certain; until he had proof of death to match his proof of life.

"But you may find the answers you seek there."

"We hope so, and we want more than anything to still beat Eudora Vane to South Polaris."

Tuyok growled at the thought of her.

"What is it saying?" Harriet asked.

"They're taking us to the frozen lake."

Harriet looked at him with utter astonishment, then a great smile broadened her lips. "It seems luck is back on our side. We need to return to the ship, get Felicity and Maudie and pack supplies."

Tuyok bowed his head. "*We will meet you back here.*"

With that, Tuyok leapt through the snow towards the other thought-wolves. Arthur heard a rush of thoughts from the other thought-wolves before they disappeared, as though the wolves could choose who around them could hear their thoughts.

When Arthur and Harriet arrived back in the clearing, Maudie gave him her death stare and marched right over, finger pointing and yelling at him. "What were you thinking? You could've got lost or worse! At least Harriet was quick enough to go after you. You could've been eaten by the beasts. Wait – why are you grinning?" She stamped on his foot.

"OWWW! I'm trying to explain... Maud, we met the beasts, except they're not beasts, they're thought-wolves and they're nothing like we've been led to believe. They're amazing. They speak through their thoughts, and I can understand what they mean. Their pack-leader, Tuyok, spoke to me and said Eudora killed some of them last time. They've never harmed a human, so that means..."

"Stop talking so fast! You're telling me you've

spoken to wolves?" She gave Harriet a sideways glance. "He must've hit his head pretty hard. . ."

"It's true," said Harriet. "Incredible, unbelievable, but true."

"So the wolves definitely didn't kill Dad and the crew?"

He shook his head.

"And you know this because they speak to you through their thoughts?"

"They're sapient creatures, but unlike any sapient creature in the First or Second Continents. They show a higher level of understanding. It's as though they've taken it to a whole new level. They can actually talk to us."

"That's pretty amazing, Arty," she said, her eyes telling him she still doubted it.

"And they're going to take us further."

Maudie paused, then shrugged and said, "What are we waiting for?"

Quickly they packed for the journey. Felicity was more than pleased to be coming along but first insisted on taking Welby through the fine details of how to feed the remaining crew and how to ration.

"I am well versed in this kind of affair, Madame," he said, raising his great eyebrows.

Harriet spoke with Forbes, Gilly and the others, giving advice and instructions on what could work, and drawing hurried plans.

They dressed warmly and packed rations, tools and essentials into backpacks. Parthena circled above, keen to get going. Queenie tottered out from the wreckage of the *Aurora*. "Prrrwt?"

Harriet picked her up and stroked her thick fur. "I'm sorry, dearest, but you need to stay here and look after Welby and the others."

The four explorers said their goodbyes to the rest of the crew and disappeared into the darkness of the forest.

Tuyok and his pack were lying together in the snow where Harriet and Arthur had left them, keeping each other warm. When he saw Arthur, Tuyok stood and stretched out his paws.

Maudie tensed and Felicity grabbed her. "Towering teapots! Are you sure about this, Arthur Brightstorm?"

"They're really friendly." He smiled.

"They're really enormous," Felicity said shakily.

Maudie frowned. "I can hear thoughts – words – someone else's, in my head! Well, it's all a bit jumbled, but that's weird."

"What are you meaning by that, flower? I can't hear anything apart from my knees knocking," Felicity said.

Harriet looked thoughtful. "Interesting – of the four of us, it seems it's just you two. Perhaps young minds are more open to such things?"

"Take it slowly, Maud. If it's too fast, ask them to slow down. It gets easier with every sentence. Sometimes they all talk and it gets a bit confused, and sometimes it's as though they are able to block everything else out and can direct a thought only to you."

"Let's get going. Do they lead the way and we walk behind?" Harriet asked.

"*There will be no need to walk. You will ride with us,*" Tuyok said.

Arthur and Maudie both grew wide-eyed and grinned.

"We aren't walking – we're riding," Arthur said. Tuyok dipped the front of his body to the snow and Arthur swung his leg over his great shoulders and climbed on to his strong back. It was soft and warm, like hugging a great carpet.

Arthur rode pure white Tuyok, Harriet, a muscular, silky brown wolf called Sangilak. Felicity rode Kinapak, a white wolf with grey patches around her eyes like a mask and big padding feet which went well with Felicity's own. Maudie went with Slartok who was midnight black – they looked a breathtaking pair with their fierce stares.

"*Ready?*" said Tuyok, and the instant Arthur thought "yes", they took off, charging through the great snowy forest.

CHAPTER 21

GRAVE NEWS

Arthur held on as best he could, with his hand clutching Tuyok's fur, as the thought-wolves ran. After a minute, Tuyok was in his thoughts, telling Arthur to relax and feel Tuyok's movements. Although it was difficult at first, Arthur began to read the landscape ahead with Tuyok, leaning into the turns and bracing for leaps. After a while they became one. Glimpses of Parthena wove through the treetops as they darted between pines – she flew ahead or above the pack, but keeping low so not to risk being seen by the *Victorious*.

They rode through the day into the short night,

covering fifty miles in one day. The thought-wolves hardly paused for breath, the relentless thud and thrust of their huge paws sending flurries of snow-dust in their wake. As the short night drew in and the sky darkened to indigo, the temperature dropped and large flakes of snow tumbled between the pines. Arthur was glad of being able to sink his hand deep into Tuyok's fur and share the warmth of his body. The rhythmic pace of the thought-wolf began to make him tired. He couldn't even remember when he'd last slept. "*Rest*," Tuyok thought, and the pack slowed and stopped.

The humans climbed down from their thought-wolves and stretched out their limbs. Now stationary, the snow soon settled on their fur hoods and eyelids. Tuyok dug snow from the bottom of nearby trees as though looking for something. He settled on a great old pine on the edge of a slope with much of its roots exposed. Tuyok deftly dug out any snow and earth with the other wolves to form an entrance and widened the cavity underneath, while Arthur, Maudie and Harriet collected needled branches to make a canopy roof. Felicity started a small fire then went deeper into the undergrowth with her wolf, Kinapak, who was digging and snouting through the dense vegetation. They had soon gathered a small pile of grubs to cook. Arthur felt so hungry he didn't even question what they were eating, but Felicity had an extraordinary ability to turn the most unappetizing food into a banquet with a sprinkling of the herbs and spices she had brought along in small vials. The wolves liked their grubs raw and couldn't see the point of ruining them with heat and bits of leaves. Dessert was honeybread flats, crumbly from the crash but delicious, and washed down with sweet tea which warmed them from the inside out.

Harriet laughed. "Even now, we have tea."

"Well, we're not animals," huffed Felicity. "No offence," she added quickly, stroking Kinapak's furry white head.

Exhausted, the humans crawled into the root den, and the thought-wolves became an insulating skirt at the bottom of the tree. They drifted to sleep in moments, eight forest creatures snuggled into a nest.

The dark night was only three chimes long, and Arthur woke to broad daylight and the soft clanks of

Felicity cooking, the smell of porridge, and Harriet and Maudie talking co-ordinates. His iron arm was making the skin around his shoulder sore because he'd had it on for so long now, but there was no way he was undressing in the cold to take it off. The snow had stopped and left the trees heavy and the forest floor dense with a fresh layer. Everything sparkled in the morning light.

"Morning, sleepy, we've been awake for ages. The thought-wolves are hunting rodents, but they'll be back soon," Maudie said.

"By ages she means moments," Felicity said, hugging Maudie to her.

"Slartok says we'll be out of the forest by the end of the day," Maudie said.

"That's brilliant. Have I got time to write before we leave?" he asked. Harriet replied that they did, so he took out his explorer journal and wrote several pages on the thought-wolves.

"You look happy," Harriet said.

He was. They were so close to Dad's ship and the frozen lake now.

The thought-wolves returned and the humans quickly ate a lucky spoonful of porridge each, climbed back on their wolves, and were soon darting and dashing between pines once more.

After half a day, the forest thinned and the trees were barren and withered, and were spread wider. The freezing wind picked up and slapped at their cheeks. Arthur rode Tuyok close to his body, burying his face in his fur whenever he could to keep warm.

Arthur's body jolted forward as the wolves came to an abrupt stop. Parthena landed on a treetop not far away and screeched a mournful cry. The thought-wolves talked between themselves in hurried thoughts.

"*Bad snow.*"

"*We can't go.*"

"*We go around.*"

"*What is it?*" Arthur asked.

A clearing could be seen through the trees ahead. The explorers climbed from the thought-wolves' backs and the four of them walked closer. There were undulations covered by snow. At first, Arthur thought they were natural mounds, but then he saw they were too regularly shaped and about the length of . . . a person. His feet rooted to the earth and sickness churned in his throat. They looked like graves. Arthur sank to his knees before the first one, feeling numb. To think one could be his dad, buried in the cold earth with the rest of his crew.

"Thirteen of the poor things," Felicity said.

They sat in silence before the graves.

"Did you say thirteen?" Arthur said suddenly, looking at Felicity. "The Brightstorm crew had fourteen – and that included Dad."

"You're right, Arty," Maudie said.

"It makes sense," Felicity said. "Someone must have dug these graves."

"Then who's missing?" said Harriet.

CHAPTER 22

GHOST SKY-SHIP

They made wreaths from twisted branches and laid them on the graves. Harriet gave a speech about bravery and finding justice, but Arthur could barely hear because his mind buzzed with unanswered questions. Harriet took a photograph, saying it may be important later, for evidence, and that Arthur should write an account in his explorer's journal, when he felt up to it.

As they walked back to the thought-wolves, Maudie whispered, "What do you think happened?"

Arthur shook his head. "Whatever it was, I'm hoping we'll find out more on the ship. If it was some sort of accident, why would the crew have been buried here, way out of sight, and not near the ship? Someone was trying to hide them. Eudora Vane thinks she's stopped us reaching this far. Let's find out what she's been trying to hide."

They were at the forest edge, the only sound the haunting whistle of the wind through the trees.

"*We are here, cub,*" said Tuyok.

The four explorers shuffled through the last of the trees and stood staring ahead.

An enormous white expanse spread before them, the late sun giving it a blue appearance – the great Frozen Lake. It was encircled east, south and west by giants of mountains, fearsome and intimidating with great jagged points of razor teeth in tight formation.

Harriet passed her binoscope to Arthur. "Look."

The *Victorious* was nestled at the forest edge in the east, golden lights shining in its portholes.

"Not even her great ship can make it over those mountains. No balloon can take the altitude," said Maudie. "And who knows what lies beyond."

Harriet nodded in agreement. "Quite right. They'll be preparing for the next stage on foot. This is where the competition becomes even, no matter who you are – just you and your ability to tough it through the cold and find a way forward. This is where we gain the upper hand." Harriet had already taken out her compass and other instruments from her belt and began taking readings and recording them in her book with Maudie.

Arthur, however, was scanning the great plain, looking desperately for the *Violetta*. Parthena looped west, then dived from the sky and landed in front of him. "Best stay low now. We don't want her catching sight of you and giving us away," he said. She let out a screech and sailed low over the snow, westwards again.

Then he spotted a curious mound of snow not far from them – he couldn't believe he'd missed it. "It's Dad's ship," he said, his heart thumping. "Parthena, you were trying to tell us!"

Harriet and Maudie stopped with their calculations and looked.

"Well, it will certainly prove a useful shelter," said Harriet. "The light is fading fast and the short night will be there soon."

"We'll skirt around the edge of the forest a little

way, so she doesn't see us, then move swiftly across to your father's sky-ship, rest there for a short time and get some sleep. It doesn't seem the Vane party has left for the mountains yet. Let's not lose the advantage."

"Will you be all right seeing your father's ship, twinnies?" Felicity circled them in her arms.

They nodded.

Arthur couldn't wait to get there; since seeing the thirteen graves he had one hope in his mind – that Dad had somehow survived and was on the *Violetta*.

"There are only ghosts there, cub," said Tuyok, reading Arthur's thoughts. But Arthur didn't want to hear it and pushed the thought away. He had to hang on to the hope.

"Can you ask how much further the thought-wolves can take us, Arthur?" said Harriet.

"The forest is our territory. We will take you to the ghost sky-ship, then we must get back to the rest of our pack. I hope you understand," said Tuyok.

"You've done more than enough, thank you."

"Be careful – the lake is restless ice, always changing and moving. Listen to it well. We will stay

with you until morning." Tuyok bowed his head. Arthur couldn't help but put his arm around the thought-wolf's great neck to feel his soft fur against his cheek, and wish that he could stay in the protection of Tuyok for ever.

"*You are welcome in our pack any moon,*" said Tuyok.

"The thought-wolves can take us to the *Violetta*, but they must get back to the rest of their pack at first light."

"We understand, thank you." Harriet patted her thought-wolf.

Arthur looked at the vast lake ahead and the mountains and felt as though he'd shrunk to the size of an insect. "So South Polaris is beyond those mountains?"

"Yes," Harriet said. "We must find a way through."

"And just the small matter of getting across this ridiculously unstable, iced-up lake, then," said Felicity.

"Yes, but that's tomorrow's problem. Right now, we make sure we stay out of sight of the *Victorious* and get some sleep."

They wove back through the trees westward, staying hidden, then the thought-wolves rode them across the short distance to the great white mound. The *Violetta* was crushed and tilted, frozen into the ground with great walls of snow banked against the sides. It looked as though it had become one with the landscape. The four of them looked up at the once beautiful sky-ship. Maudie and Arthur remembered Dad had taken them to the docks when she was being built. Arthur used to run his hand along the rails when visiting the ship; now they were rusted and broken.

"I'll climb up and check the top," said Harriet, clambering up the bank of snow.

Arthur took a step closer to Maudie.

"It's not too bad on the deck. Most of the snow has drifted to the bottom, and I think with a little digging we can get the hatch open," Harriet called.

"I'll go and help; you two wait here a moment." Near the top of the bank, Felicity took her spoon and scooped snow away from the side to reveal words: THE VIOLETTA. She looked down. "She was a beauty and no mistaking it. Graceful shapes – I bet she flew well."

Arthur put his hand to his chest and felt for the locket.

"I'm nearly through. Would you like us to look first? You know . . . in case?" Harriet asked.

"Yes," Maudie said, her voice cracking.

They waited outside for several excruciating minutes, snuggled into the fur of the thought-wolves beside the ship.

Soon, Harriet and Felicity were back, looking over the side of the deck and calling them on board.

"It's all right, there's no one here," said Harriet.

Arthur's heart sank again, and Tuyok opened his emerald eyes and looked at him. "*Be strong.*"

"It's as though everything was abandoned. It's the strangest thing," said Felicity.

Arthur and Maudie left the thought-wolves, who said they would sleep the short night outside the ship, and Arthur felt glad they were staying close for a while longer. The light was fading fast as the sun set. Harriet lit a candle and Arthur drew a long breath before following Harriet, Felicity and Maudie down the hatch and below deck.

A layer of ice frosted everything. Floorboards creaked in the eerie still as though complaining about being disturbed. Directly on the left, a door was wedged open. It led into a compact galley with a relatively large dining table for the amount of space. It looked as though everyone had left suddenly. Dirty plates were stacked in the bucket sink, and on the table, abandoned bowls sat with spoons either in them or to the sides, with small chunks of something frozen in them.

"How peculiar," said Felicity. She picked some up and sniffed.

"There are fourteen chairs," Arthur said, picking up the one closest to him and placing it upright. He scoured the table – one place didn't have a bowl.

Felicity brushed a layer of dusty ice off the work surface with her finger. "The galley was all cleared up. Perhaps they were eating something from the stores?"

"Well, I say we take a look around the rest of the ship, then sleep on it. There are bunks below – they're frosted, but it'll be better than being outside. We can't risk lighting the fires or the *Victorious* will see us," said Harriet, moving to the door.

"The fuel stores!" Arthur said suddenly.

Maudie said. "What do you think we'll find there?"

"Think about it: if the Brightstorm crew did steal the fuel from the *Victorious*, they would have excess amounts in their hold."

"Good thinking, Arthur," Harriet said. "The *Victorious* crew never said anything about taking fuel from this ship before heading back. But . . . what if what we find matches their story? Are you prepared for that?"

"He wouldn't have done it," Arthur said.

"Then let's go and see."

Felicity paused at the work surface, sniffing something.

Maudie huffed. "Come on, I hardly think it matters what their last pudding was, Felicity."

But Felicity turned, wide-eyed. "Actually, I think it matters quite a lot, twinnies. There's a tingling in my toes and a smell to this food that I don't like. There's a tinge of something bitter, masked well by sweetness, but if my instinct serves me, I'd say there's something strange."

"Are you suggesting foul play?" Harriet said.

Arthur's whole body tensed.

"I can't be sure, but..."

Arthur and Maudie looked at each other. "Do you think they were poisoned?"

"Perhaps, but surely not by their own cook?" said Felicity.

"I doubt it, but evidence as to who did it will be difficult to come by. Take what's left with us. Maybe Gilly will be able to identify what plant was used, or we may be able to test it back in Lontown," said Harriet. "Let's search the rest of the ship and take a look at those fuel stores."

They worked their way down through the ship, which revealed nothing further, then moved on to the fuel stores at the bottom.

The sides of the ship were crushed in with the pressure of the surrounding ice, but they could still see instantly that the fuel stores were completely empty.

Arthur felt a weight lift from his chest. Dad hadn't stolen any fuel. "So, someone else stole it from the *Victorious* in the Second Continent or..."

"Or Eudora Vane and her crew made up the story," said Maudie.

Harriet took some photographs for evidence.

"If any fuel was stolen, I'd say it was stolen from here."

Tired and cold, they moved to the bunk room, gathered as many blankets and quilts as they could find and piled them on top of themselves. The others fell asleep while Arthur wrote the day's events in his expedition log. Eventually he shut the book and blew out the candle. The soft sleeping breaths of the others were loud in the night, chuffing into the freezing air. His thoughts rolled around in his brain as he lay on his icy bed, feeling cold to the core.

"I can't sleep," Maudie whispered.

"Me neither."

"I can't believe the cook would have poisoned them."

"That's because the cook didn't."

"Well, who else would've been cooking for them? I heard Harriet say to Felicity that it could be the fourteenth – the missing person."

"But think about it, Maud – that theory makes no sense. What motive would someone have to kill their own crew and ruin their chances of getting back? And then bother to go and bury them all?"

"Yes, there is that, I suppose."

And then Arthur realized. He sat bolt upright.

"What is it?" Maudie whispered.

"The fourteenth – the missing grave, it's Dad. I know for certain he wasn't one of the thirteen poisoned."

"How could you possibly know? You're just saying that because you're hoping he's alive. Wait . . . you're not thinking it was him?"

"Of course not, don't be so daft! But I know he didn't eat the pudding – the empty space with only a cup was his."

"How could you possibly know that?"

"Dad was allergic to eggs, like me. He was always so careful about what he ate. It looked cake-like, so he wouldn't have eaten the pudding."

Maudie paused for a long time. "Genius, Arty!"

"And I still think it was Eudora Vane."

"But she was on another ship."

"Think about it – if they reached here at around the same time they would have a short time to prepare for the next stage on foot. Eudora could have come to visit – a friendly gesture before they set off to race to the Polaris. Maybe she poisoned the crew to stop them going any further or to get a head start through the mountain. But whether she intended to kill them or not, she made up the beast story to cover her tracks, paid her crew to keep quiet, and came back to Lontown after it went wrong."

Maudie remained silent for a moment. "All right, that makes perfect sense – except to convict her in Lontown, we need proof, and we still don't know what happened to Dad."

"That's why we're going across to the *Victorious*. Right now."

CHAPTER 23

THE PLAN

Arthur pushed back the layers of quilts and swung his feet as soundlessly as possible out of the bunk.

"What do you think we'll find?" Maudie whispered.

"Some evidence that Eudora Vane is behind this, that she sent the poisoned cakes over. We've found Dad's ship, but it doesn't add up to anything that could work in court. This is our last chance to find out more. Unless we have more proof, she'll get away with it."

"But shouldn't we wake Harriet and Felicity and come up with a plan?"

"Of course not. Harriet has already ruled out going anywhere near the *Victorious*. They won't agree to going. We'll be back before they wake – they'll never know."

"But. . ."

"We're wasting time, come on." Parthena was sleeping on the end of Arthur's bunk. She opened one eye. "Stay here," Arthur whispered.

Arthur took Harriet's camera, then hurried on to the deck, closely followed by Maudie.

Outside, Tuyok was waiting for them. "*You may walk softly, but your thoughts were loud enough to wake me.*"

"*Please don't try to stop us.*"

"*I see you are determined, so I'm here to offer my help.*"

Arthur and Maudie rode Tuyok across the snow plain on the outskirts of the lake towards the *Victorious*. The night was deathly still and quiet, apart from the creaks and groans of the frozen lake, and two young explorers on a great wolf, outlined in moonlight, riding across the expanse of night.

They reached the *Victorious*.

"Thank you," Arthur thought, climbing down with Maudie.

"I will wait for you," Tuyok said.

They crept across the snow and towards the great hulk of wood and metal. Silently they climbed up the side ladder, and tiptoed across deck to the hatch.

Maudie found the catch and, with a careful click, it released. "She wouldn't suspect anyone would be mad enough to break in," she whispered.

The sickly sweet smell of perfume wafted through the hatch. They both froze but it was silent inside.

"We've definitely got the right ship," Arthur said, swallowing to stop a sneeze. They started down the steps.

Maudie grabbed his arm. "Wait! How do we know which room to try?"

"*Exploring in the Third Age* – chapter fifteen. The basic layout of sky-ships is pretty much the same across all families. The sleeping quarters and stores will be on the lowest deck, galley and dining port side, the library and captain's room starboard."

Maudie stared at him for a moment, impressed. Then she said, "OK, let's start in the captain's room. If there's anything to be found, that's where it'll be."

"My thoughts precisely."

When they were sure all was still silent, they lit a candle to see their way, then continued down the steps into a hallway lavishly decorated with carved wooden panels. Arthur ran his fingers across twines and roses. "It's part of the Vane explorer symbol," he whispered.

Maudie curled her nostril and stuck out her tongue. "*Vile* explorers, more like."

On the right-hand side, the first door was huge, with a large crystal doorknob. The letters EV were carved elegantly into the wood. Arthur put his ear close to the door to check for any noises beyond. He turned the handle. Inside, the floor felt soft underfoot. A pink fur rug was laid out at the entrance and in the middle of the room stood a glass table with diamonds embedded in the edges.

"Her initials are engraved on everything, Arty. It's as though she wants to put her stamp on the entire Wide." Maudie picked up a pink paperweight with EV engraved in fancy letters. A teacup and saucer was laid out next to it, also embossed with EV, even the little silver teaspoon.

Maudie ran her hand across the bookshelves.

"Maybe she has a book on poisons; that could be evidence, right?"

"Good thinking. You search them, and I'll see what's in these boxes." They were of all shapes and sizes: pink pearl, crystal, silver. He carefully placed the candle on the shelf and opened the nearest to him. It was full of tiny pink shells, the next was full of pearls, another with a pungent pink spice that smelt the same as Eudora's perfume. He stifled another sneeze and put the lid on.

"Oh, look, here's one on toxic plants. Maybe she made notes in it or something."

"Hm?" Arthur opened a small silver box. What was inside halted him – he stared for a moment. It was a silver locket. His hand reached for the locket around his neck. It was still there. "Maud, this locket looks just like Dad's – it even has VE inscribed, not EV?"

"She would've probably had the engraver killed for that mistake."

"No, I think it's meant to be like that." He traced his fingers across the silver engraving. The V and the E were delicately entwined so that the line of the V wound three times around the stem of the E.

"Maudie, it's identical. There must have been two – one for Violetta and one for Ernest. The cheek of the woman; she must have stolen it from Dad." He took the matching locket and looped it around his neck.

Maudie let out a gasp that made him look up. "You won't believe this!"

"You've found an engineering book you haven't read?" he whispered sarcastically.

"This is not a time for jokes, Arty."

She smiled and turned the large volume around. "I do believe we have all the evidence we need. Who's the genius now?" she crowed.

Inside, the pages were glued together into a solid piece with a central rectangular cavity that held a set of finely crafted drawers. The fronts were covered with coloured paper and fitted with carved frames and silver knobs. Handwritten paper labels gave the names of different poisonous plants – castor oil, valerian, thorn apple and deadly nightshade.

"Look!" Maudie unfolded a piece of paper. It was a handwritten recipe for cakes, with calculations and quantities of nightshade added in a different ink.

Excitement rippled through him. "It must have been her. Let's take a photograph and get out of here. Lay it out on the table beside the initialled casket. Here, place the candle there for light."

"And we'll tell the police where this is when we're all back in Lontown, and let her try to explain it away!"

Arthur laid the book on the table and Maudie took a photograph.

Then something brushed past Arthur's foot and scurried in front of him – he jolted and his arm bashed into the table, knocking the teacup. It rattled to the side. Maudie lunged for it but was too late. It smashed on the wooden floor. They looked at each other with eyes as round as the moon.

"It was only a rat, Arty! What's the matter with you?" Maudie quickly blew out the candle and tugged him to the door.

"I'm sorry, I couldn't help it!"

"Let's hope no one heard," she said, glaring at him.

But as they reached the hallway a clonk sounded below and a sharp female voice called, "Who's up there?"

With a panicked look, they ran for the stairs.

CHAPTER 24

EVIDENCE

Footsteps thundered below. They scrambled and slipped along the hallway in their panic to get away. Doors banged, followed by shouts and more feet running. Maudie led the way up the stairs and urged him on. Arthur gasped a cold breath of air as she yanked him on deck.

They ran to the side but couldn't see the rope ladder. "Where is it?" he said, panicked. Then Arthur saw the glint of Tuyok's eyes shining green in the dark further along. "Come on. It's back here!"

Footsteps clattered up the steps.

"You go first, Maudie."

"Not on your life. You go," she snapped, pushing him forward.

Arthur swung his leg over the side when the unmistakable click of a gun being cocked froze him.

Slowly, they turned and winced at the bright light on them.

They recognized the sneering, slimy voice of Bartemaus Smethwyck. "Well, if it isn't the Brightstorm twins," he said as though their name was infected.

Eudora Vane appeared, pristine in pink silk pyjamas. A man followed behind and put a pink fur coat over Eudora's shoulders. "What a surprise. If you'd wanted an invitation, you only needed to ask." She ran a hand down Arthur's cheek. "Now, what are you doing on my sky-ship?"

"Let us go," Arthur said through gritted teeth.

"The theft of equipment and supplies, perhaps? Yet there is nothing in your hands. Or hand. How curious."

Smethwyck lifted his gun.

"Perhaps there is no need for force, Smethwyck – they appear to be alone. Why not come down into the warmth – we can all still be friends."

"We're not going anywhere with you," Maudie snapped and linked Arthur's arm.

"*You* killed the crew of the *Violetta*," Arthur said.

Madame Vane shook her head. "Poor, deluded boy. Losing your father has softened your brain. They were ravaged by wolves. It's futile to doubt it."

"There are thirteen graves in the forest."

Her eyes narrowed. "What are you talking about?"

"The crew were fourteen, but there are thirteen graves. What happened to my father?"

"You're mistaken."

"You poisoned the crew, Eudora."

"Don't be absurd."

Maudie stepped beside him. "And we've got the evidence to prove it!"

"Probably not the best moment to say that," Arthur whispered.

The muscles in Eudora's face tightened and the mask fell away. She looked them up and down. "Your father was a disgrace. He didn't understand his place; he thought he could force his way into explorer society, and he deserved everything he got."

Arthur's stomach churned with anger, but the

gun was still pointed at them. Then he heard faint scratching on the side of the ship. He coughed loudly trying to cover up the noise.

"Smethwyck, take them below. Shoot if they try anything."

Smethwyck waved the gun at them, indicating the direction in which they were to go.

Arthur exchanged a look with Maudie, trying to tell her not to move.

The scratching came again. The silver insect flying above Eudora turned to the noise.

"Whatever is it, Miptera?" Eudora said.

In a flash, Tuyok leapt on to the deck, his huge body shining white in the moonlight, batting away Miptera with his great paw. The crew jumped back as Tuyok's hackles raised and he let out a great snarl. "*I hear her thoughts. She means to kill you both if you go below.*"

Smethwyck still had his gun on Arthur and Maudie, but his attention was on Tuyok.

"*Snow is soft behind. I will distract them. Jump, cubs!*"

Tuyok let out another vicious snarl and braced to attack. Arthur and Maudie ran for the back of the ship and leapt. With a thud, they tumbled across the snow.

The darkness filled with shouts and vicious growls.

"Tuyok!" Arthur shouted.

"*Run, cubs!*"

A single shot echoed into the night.

"*Tuyok!*" Arthur thought desperately. There was no reply.

They paused looking up at the *Victorious*. Arthur called again.

Maudie grabbed his arm. "There's nothing we can do."

Another shot sent snow skittering upward beside Arthur's feet. They ran, slipping and falling in the snow. Shouts weren't far behind.

"Faster, Arty!"

A black shape appeared, black paws hurtling towards them. It was Slartok.

"They killed him!" Arthur cried.

"*Come – I will take you.*"

A voice echoed through the night. "You can run, Brightstorms, but it's hopeless! Your sky-ship is in pieces; you can't get back. You won't survive long, especially when winter sets in. If you think it's cold now, you're in for a treat!"

They climbed on to Slartok and charged back towards the *Violetta*.

As they reached it, Harriet stood on the deck, a candle lit, her expression confused and panicked. "We were woken by the thought-wolves howling and shots in the distance. What in all the continents has happened?"

Arthur and Maudie climbed up the bank of snow.

"You scared the life out of us!" Felicity said.

"We went to look for evidence," Maudie said.

"Don't blame her, it was my idea." Arthur rubbed tears back with his fist.

Harriet's confusion turned to anger. "Evidence?"

Arthur took the locket from his neck. His voice shook. "Parthena brought this back. Dad never took it off. We knew there was more to what happened right from the start. We wanted to bring honour back to our name by finding the truth out here, not just reaching South Polaris."

"And you didn't think to mention that to me?"

"We thought it would ruin our chances of coming along."

She shook her head and paced in quick strides. "Going to the *Victorious* alone was incredibly stupid – you should've woken us and discussed it before you took it upon yourself. Now Eudora Vane is on to us and we've lost all element of surprise. This isn't only about you two!"

"I wasn't thinking," Arthur said.

"That's the problem – neither of you were."

"I'm sorry! Tuyok's dead, and it was my fault because he was trying to help us." Guilt smothered him. He couldn't breathe.

Harriet fell silent, then she huffed out a long breath. "Whoever shot Tuyok was a monster – it wasn't your fault they pulled the trigger. They had a choice too."

"They're coming for us, Harriet, because we found the evidence – Eudora had a book on toxic plants, and a recipe for poison cakes. We took photographs." Maudie passed her the camera.

"*And* you took my camera?" Harriet said.

"We're sorry, truly," Maudie said.

"I knew there had to be a reason for the tingling in my toes in the galley!" Felicity said.

Harriet shook her head angrily. She took her

binoscope from her belt and looked across the snowy plain. "There's no sign of them. They must have turned back, probably to get more weapons. We need to leave at once and cross the lake to the mountains – we'll be less exposed there."

"But we won't see the cracks in the ice so well in the dark," said Felicity.

"We don't have a choice." Harriet glared at Arthur and Maudie, who both looked at their feet. Then she tutted and sighed. "I just wish you'd woken me – we could have come up with a plan."

"I'm sorry," Arthur said again.

"Maudie, I thought you'd at least know better."

Arthur wasn't sure what she meant by that. Was he really that foolish?

Felicity took them by the hand. "There's nothing we can do for poor Tuyok except carry on and when the time comes, give that vile woman everything she deserves."

"Let's get packed up." Harriet paused. "That's if you both want to go on towards South Polaris? I need to go on, for the crew's sake – but the thought-wolves could take you back to the *Aurora*. You'll be safer in the forest with them. Of course, that's *if* they even want to help out any more. If I don't make it back within a moon-cycle and they've mended the ship, you can fly back to Lontown and present any evidence you have. It should be enough to prove your father's innocence."

Arthur shook his head. "No. We need to make it to South Polaris, for him."

Harriet nodded. "I thought you would say that. But you must promise me, no more secrets."

They nodded. Then they all grabbed their packs, plus food from the stores of the *Violetta* that Felicity thought was still safe to eat.

The thought-wolves listened quietly to Arthur's thoughts explaining Tuyok's fate. For a few agonizing moments, nothing was said, but then Kinapak, the wolf with grey rings around her eyes, spoke.

"Tuyok was always a wolf of great valour and generous in spirit. We will honour him by helping you as far as we can across the lake. This will give you a head start."

Arthur's heart nearly broke at this.

They moved slower across the frozen lake, stopping frequently for the wolves to sniff the air and listen to the groans of the ice. The lights coming from the

Victorious became distant and the enormous mountain peaks loomed ever bigger beneath the night sky.

"Maybe they're not coming straight after us?" Maudie said.

"We did catch her unprepared," said Felicity.

"But you can bet she'll be speeding now and will be off before daybreak," said Harriet.

After a while, a pale blue glow seeped across the sky and the stars became less bright. The thought-wolves came to a stop, still some distance from the base of the mountains, which rose to unimaginable heights before them, as if the world simply ended at a massive stone wall.

"We must leave you here and return to our pack. This is as far as we can go, as the ice may be too unsafe for our size in the rising sun."

"We understand, thank you," Arthur said. He hugged Slartok and he knew that thoughts of Tuyok weighed heavily on them both.

"Thought-wolves have a saying, cub – until we will meet once again in tomorrow's snow."

The amber glow of the rising sun shone in the east. With a lump in his throat, Arthur watched the thought-wolves head back across the ice.

CHAPTER 25

THE ICE LAKE

The last stage of the frozen lake spread before them, bright and blue, veined with white cracks and fissures. They moved cautiously but swiftly, with Harriet leading them onwards, prodding the ice as they went.

Arthur and Maudie kept glancing over their shoulders.

"Don't worry, there's still no sign of them," said Harriet.

"Which is strange, don't you think?" said Felicity.

"I do, but all we can do is worry about ourselves and keep pushing forward. Maybe they've run into a technical problem."

They carried on and after a morning's walk they were almost at the base of the mountains. The sun was at its warmest and even though the temperatures were still freezing, the ice beneath their feet had more movement to it. It cracked and groaned as though it was alive and didn't much want them there. Harriet took her compass from her belt to check the direction, while Maudie looked through her binoscope trying to find a tunnel entrance.

"I, for one, could do with a cup of tea. The sooner we get to the mountain and can start a fire, the better," said Felicity.

"I can't see anything that might be an opening." Maudie tapped the binoscope against her leg.

"Give it to me," Arthur said.

"Because you have magical eyes or something?" she tutted.

But she was right, of course. Arthur couldn't see any openings either. He gave the binoscope to Harriet.

"There's nothing obvious, but sometimes you've got to look beyond. See how those rocks over there are balanced curiously on top of one another?" She pointed and passed Arthur the binoscope.

He could see boulders piled up in one section against the sheer mountain face. "Yes," he answered.

"How do you think they got there?"

Arthur thought about it. "An avalanche at some point in the past?"

"Exactly. Which means an entrance could be hidden. There! Look at the dark patch above the pile of rocks straight ahead. That might be an entrance."

Arthur took several steps forward with the binoscope, watching the shadowed rocks, feeling as though he could almost reach out and touch them. He felt impatient to make progress. What if that small piece of hope lingering inside him was true – he knew the chances were small, but what if Dad had made it to the mountain?

An almighty crack sounded as the ice split. Arthur's feet disappeared beneath him.

Ice cold stung every part of him and flashes of white and blue were all around. His whole body felt as though it was on fire; his hand and fingers wouldn't move. A hundred things ran through his head at once, like if he kicked he might send himself further below, beneath the ice for ever. His backpack dragged him down, while the air in his iron arm made it lurch upward, but it wasn't buoyant enough to pull him back to the surface. He tried not to panic or breathe, but his body gasped and snatched for air and water flooded into his lungs and the pain was terrifying – then everything went dark.

The next thing he knew he was choking and spluttering, Maudie was crying, Harriet was soaked and Felicity was looking over him, pale as the ice itself.

"Oh, thank goodness!" Felicity put her hand to his cheek. Parthena landed beside him but stayed a little back, tilting her head with concern

Arthur couldn't speak. Everything hurt. Maudie pounced on him, pulling him to her in a huge hug. "You're breathing! Harriet was so quick – she saw the ice go beneath you and dived straight in."

"We need to make a fire and get you warm and dry," Harriet stuttered through chattering teeth and blue lips.

"And you too, Harriet. You'll have to let someone else take the lead for a moment," Felicity said.

Arthur felt dizzy, sick and freezing to the core.

Felicity and Maudie gathered the kit.

"Come on, this ice isn't looking good and my

feet are tingling a fair bit. We can't wait. I'll take the stick and check ahead. Can you walk, Arthur?" Felicity helped him up and put his arm around her shoulder. "I'll take your weight, twinnie."

"I'll take Harriet's equipment and help her." Maudie paused. "But where's your compass? And the binoscope?"

They froze and looked at Harriet.

"I had it in my hand – I lost it beneath," she said.

Arthur felt hollow. He'd lost them the one piece of navigational equipment that could help them find their way under the mountain, and Harriet's binoscope.

"The binoscope we can do without as I still have my uniscope," Maudie said. "But how will we find our way without the compass? The way-finder needs a horizon and stars, so that'll be absolutely useless under the mountain."

"Well, there's nothing we can do now – best not dwell on it. Let's get you both out of those wet things, or not having a compass will be the least of our worries," said Felicity.

Each step felt as though they were stepping on glass. They'd seen what could happen if they put a foot wrong. Sometimes the ice would moan beneath them and they would freeze, shuddering with cold, too scared to move forward. But Felicity led them onwards, prodding the ice before them as they went, pausing, reading the ice with her great feet until eventually they reached the edge of the mountain.

Arthur had never been so pleased to walk on rock. Felicity located the small opening, and they climbed through.

Inside, it opened into a cave. It was too dark to see how big it was, but the echo of Felicity's voice travelled a long way. They unloaded their equipment not far from the entrance, where they still had a little light. Felicity's backpack was like a magic bag and she soon had all manner of things laid out on the rocky floor. She lit a fire with some dry shrubs she'd brought from the forest.

Maudie helped Harriet and Arthur out of their wet clothes and wrapped them in blankets by the fire. She silently made a makeshift line tied between rocks to dry their clothes over the fire. She took off Arthur's arm for him to dry off, removing the page folded inside and carefully adding it to the line. She rubbed the arm with a cloth by the fire, and then she said she wanted to keep an eye on the entrance in case the Vane crew arrived. She placed herself by the opening, and took the arm for further oiling and polishing.

Soon Felicity handed out tea and dried marsh cakes.

"Felicity, I can't believe you fit all this in your bag," Arthur said.

"Of course, dearie – I don't go anywhere without tea."

The warm, honeyed drink was the best thing Arthur had ever drunk. Parthena flew into the cave and nestled by his feet to warm them. The feeling in his toes and fingers slowly returned, and Arthur was soon sleeping, with Harriet fast asleep beside him.

When he next woke, the tunnel had darkened. Maudie and Felicity were now dozing by the fire.

"It's the short night again, Arthur," Harriet whispered. "You've had a good sleep, and I haven't been awake long."

But she still looked pale.

"Perhaps you should rest some more," he said.

She passed him a handful of dried fruit and

seeds to nibble on and a canister of water. "I'll let you into a secret, Arthur. I'm not very good at sitting still for too long."

"I'd noticed."

They both smiled.

"Maudie and Felicity did a good job of sorting the equipment and drying the clothes, and the oilskin lining of your bag managed to keep the contents pretty dry." She handed him his explorer's journal.

Arthur flicked through the pages that now had damp marks around the edges, but the writing was intact.

"I've taken a quick look ahead and the cavern opens out even more. There's a good chance the cave system goes straight through the mountain. These appear to be the ancient volcanic chambers and lava tubes I had hoped we'd find here."

He raised his eyebrows.

"It's all right, the thermal activity seems minimal; I don't think there's a threat."

Maudie's eyes flickered open. "How are you feeling?"

"Better, thanks," he said.

She nodded, but there was a strange tightness to her expression. She flipped over to face away.

"What's the matter? I said I'm all right."

Maudie sat up. "I'm angry with you, Arthur. In fact, I'm flipping furious."

"What?"

"I'll check the entrance," said Harriet, leaving them.

Felicity snored.

Maudie's whisper was quiet but fierce. "It's always about you and what you want."

"What the clinking cogs are you going on about?"

"You nearly died on that lake."

"I didn't exactly fall in on purpose."

"But you weren't looking properly or thinking. You had your eye on what you wanted. Like when you dashed off alone in the forest, and when you decided to go to the *Victorious*. You were only thinking of yourself and how you wanted to do things."

"What do you mean? You want to find out the truth as much as I do."

"Yes, but not at the risk of everything. Making a stupid decision cost poor Tuyok his life."

"You know I feel terrible about Tuyok." Arthur looked away, his chest tight.

"Do you know why I came on this expedition?"

"To find out what really happened and to clear the Brightstorm name, of course."

She shook her head and drew a long breath. "I came because I know what it means to you, Arty. I knew you would do this anyway, whatever I said, and I couldn't bear to lose the only family I've got left in this world. You're so relentless in your need for the truth, I had no choice."

"Don't be silly, of course you wanted to."

"I do want the truth, but not at any cost. My legacy to Mum and Dad's memory is to stay alive and show that some good came of them. To restore the Brightstorm name to greatness by making my mark on the world. You've been hanging on to this thought that somehow he might have survived, but we both know that was a fool's hope. It's been over a year; you've seen what it's like here, and it's not even the depths of winter."

Harriet glanced over her shoulder at them.

Arthur felt dreadful – he'd been so wrapped up in himself he hadn't even thought to consider what

Maudie wanted. He'd just assumed – they were twins after all. But as he thought back he realized there had been times she had tried to tell him, he just hadn't wanted to hear her. After a long silence, Arthur crawled across and hugged her. "I'm sorry."

She nodded. "Don't get me wrong, part of me loves what we're doing too. But it's always been on your terms, and you need to consider others more." She stood up, straightened her oilskin jacket and brushed down her trousers. "Let me help you with your arm. Your shoulder probably needs balm where it rubs and I need to oil the hinges again or they'll seize, and it needs a polish."

"I don't know what I'd do without you, Maud."

"Or me you." She paused. "And one more thing."

"Anything."

"Can you stop this habit of falling into dangerous things? It's not good for my nerves!"

They laughed and Felicity suddenly snored so loudly she woke herself. She looked around flustered. "Something occurring, twinnies? Harriet, what are you doing keeping watch – you should be resting."

"I'm fine, Miss Wiggety. Arthur and I have both

slept and I'm keen we keep our advantage over the Vane crew."

"So what next?" said Arthur.

Harriet re-joined them. "If the inside of this mountain is an enormous system of ancient lava tubes and caverns, I'm sure there's a good chance we could make it all the way through."

Arthur sighed. "Except now we don't have a compass, and as Maudie said, the way-finder is useless without stars and a horizon to guide us."

"We could get lost and go around in circles for days," Felicity said.

Arthur thought for a moment. There was always a way. "If we could choose the routes going in the most southerly direction, we would stand a better chance of finding a way out to the other side. We don't have a compass, but what if we could make one." Arthur looked at Maudie.

Maudie drifted into the thoughtful faraway look she always got when she was engineering, because the seeing was happening in her brain. She drummed her fingers on the stone floor. After a moment she said, "If only we had a pin and some water."

“We will likely find pools in the chambers leading off here, if that helps?” said Harriet.

Maudie nodded. “But we still need an iron pointer.”

Their thoughts collided. They all looked at Arthur’s iron arm.

“Genius,” they said together.

CHAPTER 26

UNDER THE MOUNTAIN

They couldn't wait to pack up and find the first cavern with a water pool to try out the idea. First, they made a longer-lasting torch-fire, using special sap which Harriet had brought, spread on to wrapped up strips of clothes they'd sacrificed. Harriet took charge of marking their way by arranging small stones into the shape of arrows at the entrances so that they would be able to find the way back. They made their way through several tunnels before they entered a huge cavern. It took Arthur's breath away. Great stalagmites rose from the floor and enormous stalactites loomed above.

Thousands of tiny blue lights illuminated the cave ceiling – it was like entering a magical underground world.

"What is it?" he breathed.

In a ripple, the light vanished, leaving the glow of their torch-fire.

Harriet thought for a moment. "Just let me put the torch back around the corner, if these are what I think..."

As she did, the light from the torch-fire faded. Slowly, the lights above pricked back to life.

"I think they're tiny creatures, like those found in the caves of the Galabela mountains of the Second Continent – glow-worms."

"Extraordinary," said Felicity.

"But how would they survive in here?" Maudie asked.

The soft flow of water rippled musically through the cave.

"There's probably some thermal activity deep within the mountain. There are likely active minerals and tiny creatures in the water for the glow-worms to feed on."

It was amazing, as though they'd found a secret

life system. The thrill of it tingled inside Arthur, making him forget everything that had happened. All that existed was this wonderful place and the feeling that they were glimpsing something no one had before, as though nature had given them a secret pass.

"It's a privilege, isn't it?" Harriet said. She patted him gently on the shoulder.

"We'd better try out our theory," Maudie said.

Arthur took off his jacket and unhitched his iron arm, while Harriet retrieved the torch-fire.

"It's a bit different to a pin," Felicity said.

"But hollow – it should float and it'll always point towards the magnetic south," Maudie said.

"But how?" Harriet asked.

"I magnetized the arm when I made it, as I thought it would be useful for picking things up."

"You are a very surprising pair." Harriet laughed.

"Come on – what are we waiting for!" said Felicity, shuffling her feet.

Maudie placed the iron arm in a still pool away from the flowing stream. They waited for a painful moment while nothing happened. Slowly it began drifting around until it settled with the pointed finger to the left of the cavern.

"Well, it looks like that way is south," said Maudie. She retrieved the arm and they chose the most southerly tunnel. They went onwards through the ancient lava tubes until they found the next cavern with a pool, always keeping as southerly as they could. Onwards they went, for chime after chime through the mountain, losing track of time and direction, putting all their trust in the iron arm.

But Parthena grew more agitated as they went on, landing in front of them and frantically flapping her wings. "Not being able to see the sky must be bothering her. Do you think there's much further to go?" Arthur said.

"Well, I know how she feels," Harriet said. She certainly wasn't at ease inside the mountain, cringing at the sight of the smaller tunnels and sweat beading on her brow. "I've never liked being penned in either," she said.

When they entered a vast cavern, Felicity sat herself down on a large, flat rock. "I could do with taking the weight off my feet for a while – I feel like we've been walking day and night. I miss the sun."

"I don't miss the cold – at least it's warmer in the

mountain." Maudie took off another layer and tied it around her waist.

"There's no way to tell how far we have to go, I'm afraid. Let's set up camp for a break, and I'll go on a little to check," said Harriet.

They set down their packs and rested while Harriet went to check ahead. Parthena had disappeared high in the cavern and refused to come down, no matter how much Arthur called her and tried to tempt her with a sliver of dried fish. Eventually he gave up and took out his expedition journal. It seemed like a dream, the fact that he was in the middle of a mountain in the far reaches of the Third Continent.

Maudie and Felicity had a snooze, while Arthur wrote the most recent events in his explorer's journal. But he kept thinking back to what had happened on the *Victorious* and what Eudora had said. He shut the book and looked towards the end of the cave. Although Harriet had promised not to go far, she had been ages. Impatient, Arthur walked to the tunnel and peered inside, just as the light of her torch flame appeared somewhere at the other end.

"Arthur, is that you? You made me jump." She looked tired and her brow was deeply furrowed.

"Is everything all right?" he asked. "Do you think we might be nearly at the other side?"

She nodded, although for some reason he felt there was more.

"It's only a few tunnels away, as I suspected," she said.

As they walked back, Harriet didn't speak, and Arthur kept glancing sideways at her, trying to work out what was the matter.

"Perhaps we should wake the others," he said. "I can't wait to get back outside, even if it is deathly cold out there."

"Yes, me too, but let them sleep awhile."

They sat warming their hands by the embers still glowing where their small fire had been.

"What is it, Harriet? You look worried about something. Did you see something on the other side – did you see Eudora?"

She shook her head. "No, no. Now get a little sleep before we set off again."

Arthur lay down, drifting in and out of broken sleep. He was woken by whispers between Felicity and Harriet. A single candle flickered between them.

"You've got to tell them," Felicity said.

"I know. I just want them to be rested before they hear."

"Why, what is it?" Arthur said, sitting up.

The two women looked at each other with silent resignation, then Felicity gently shook Maudie awake. After a few awkward false starts, Harriet took a breath. "I'm so sorry, you two. I went further on in the tunnels, and . . . I've found your father."

The twins gaped at her, not understanding.

"I mean to say, I found . . . his frozen body."

The words were a punch to the chest.

Harriet took something from her bag and handed it to Arthur. It was a diary with the Brightstorm Moth emblazoned on the front. His throat constricted as though it was being squeezed by a great vice.

"He must have made it to the mountain after his crew was poisoned. He almost made it through, but he died in an ice cave not far from here," Harriet said sadly.

Arthur looked up to the rocks where Parthena

perched. “Parthena knew – that’s why she’s been so agitated. She remembers this place.”

“It’s only confirming what you already knew deep down, twinnies,” Felicity said, sitting between them and holding them tight as they cried.

They sat that way for some time. Then Harriet relit the small fire, and Felicity took cups from her backpack and tea leaves from her small purse. She added dried milk and several spoons of honey to each cup. She didn’t talk, she didn’t try to tell them that it would make everything better, although as they sat there sipping the warm sweet taste of home, it made the awfulness of reaching that point not quite as terrible.

After a while, Arthur roused himself and picked up his dad’s diary. He ran his fingers over the cover, then opened it. Inside were mostly calculations and co-ordinates, but as he turned the pages there were accounts confirming what their evidence had taught them about the poisoning.

“Would you be able to read some to us, Arthur?” Harriet asked.

Arthur nodded. He swallowed hard and began to read:

I should have known there is no such thing as goodwill when it comes to Eudora Vane.

A member of her crew brought the cakes, the likes of which the crew had not had in many weeks. Looking back, I curse myself for not realizing. The crew fell mortally ill. There was nothing I could do. Doctor Samin was the first to go – there was no remedy to stave the poison. It worked swiftly and they had perished within the chime. I took them to the forest edge and dug the frozen earth to make as best graves for each crewmember as I could, knowing the Vane crew would soon return, and I wasn't safe. From the forest, I watched them come to the Violetta, *steal our pitch and begin their search for the missing crew. I skirted the edge, hoping I could at some point make it back to the* Violetta, *as I had barely any supplies on me. But I was seen.*

Arthur paused.

"Are you all right?" Harriet said.

Felicity put an arm around him, and Maudie took the diary and continued.

I was shot at and surrounded, the only route left for me to run was across the unstable lake towards the mountains. It is a miracle I made it. They took flight in the Victorious *and shot cannons at me when I was almost at the mountains. The cannon fire set off an avalanche, destroying a huge section of the lake. I reached the mountain edge just before the rock fall, and although the mountain seemed impenetrable, at that last moment I saw a small cave entrance and scrambled to it just in time. I am sure Eudora believed I had been crushed in the avalanche. I heard the* Victorious's *engines as they searched the mountains for a way through, until they finally faded."*

"Despicable woman. And it confirms that the story about the fuel being stolen is a lie," Harriet said.

"She was forced to give up and return to Lontown," said Arthur.

Maudie passed the diary back to Arthur. "There's a little more. Will you read the last bit?"

I am lost deep in the caves, the little fuel I had on me for the torch-flame is nearly exhausted and my pencil is worn to its end. My undying hope is that someone finds my diary, and brings justice for my crew. The burning fury I have for Eudora is fuelled by my one regret that I will never get to see my beloved children grow into the marvellous adults I know they will be, and if this journal is found, my last wish is that they know my love is eternal.

The writing faded, the last words barely scratched into the page.

"You wouldn't last long being stuck here without supplies. Poor Dad," Maudie said, tears welling once more. Parthena flew from the ceiling and landed before Maudie. She hopped on to Maudie's arm and butted her head to her cheek. Maudie gasped in amazement. "She's never done that to me before – it's usually you, Arty."

The great white hawk looked at Arthur. There was such a sense of knowing in her eyes. Parthena had always carried the truth of what had happened to Dad. And Arthur understood that at that moment

Maudie needed Parthena's comfort more than he did.

"And she made it back to us, Maud. Without her bringing back the necklace, maybe we'd never have doubted Eudora's story."

"That's some bird," said Felicity. And Parthena's screech filled the cavern, as though releasing the burden she'd carried.

After a while they knew it was time to move on.

They packed up and carried onwards.

CHAPTER 27
THE SOUTHERN AURORA

It wasn't much further before the small band of explorers finally saw a glimmer of bluish, cold light, different from their torch-fire, in the tunnel ahead. They broke into a run, the rush of freezing fresh air enveloping them. With a great whoosh, Parthena flew past Arthur and out into the open.

Harriet wasn't far behind. "I can't wait to be outside again!"

But at the tunnel exit they all came to a standstill and stared open-mouthed.

It was the short night. Before them, a vast field of snow stretched out for as many miles as they could see.

But it was the view above that took their breath away. Huge waves of colour rippled in the star-speckled sky – emerald green, piercing pink, luminous orange. No one spoke as they stood in the utter quiet of winter's dusk and watched the dance of light.

"Well, that's a sight to behold, and no mistaking," whispered Felicity.

Arthur was sure he saw a tear in the corner of Harriet's eye as she whispered. "It's the southern aurora."

"Is this why you named the ship the *Aurora*?" he asked.

Harriet nodded. "I had heard the tales of those seen in the North, and I dared to hope we might see them here, but I never expected anything this beautiful."

"Dad was so close," Maudie said.

"He would have loved this." Arthur smiled.

After a while, Harriet took out the uniscope and looked across the plains. "All seems quiet. I don't believe the Vane crew have found a faster way through the mountain." She unfastened her way-finder and started manipulating it and lining it up with the horizon and the south star. "When we reach ninety degrees and the sun remains in the same place in the sky, then we will be at the exact point of South Polaris." She scribbled some calculations in her notebook, closely watched by Maudie. After a moment, Harriet smiled. "I estimate it will take no more than two days."

They hugged each other.

"Should we rest the night in the security of the mountain, or do we keep going and pitch up when we're too tired to walk another step?" The glint of adventure was in Harriet's eyes.

"I think we can go on for a few more chimes, that's if you're both all right with it?" said Felicity.

Arthur and Maudie looked at each other. They'd lost everything, but now they had the chance to complete Dad's last mission.

"Let's go," Arthur said, and they began heading down towards the great snow plain.

*

After several chimes travelling, the intense cold was getting to them. Their footsteps had become slow and laboured and they yawned and shivered, huddled into their jackets, chins to their chests. The light changed suddenly as a great bank of dark clouds raged in from the south, travelling at frightening speed. Great plumes of thick grey billowed towards them. "That doesn't look good," Harriet said, her words a teeth-chattering stammer. She looked back to the mountain and slammed the uniscope against her legs. "We should've rested there; we were too hasty, and now we're going to be caught in what could be the most vicious storm I've ever seen – and I don't fancy our chances in the tent."

They exchanged worried looks.

What would Dad do? Arthur thought. He'd always taught him to use what they had, not to focus on what you couldn't do, but what you could. But there was only snow as far as they could see. Then it came to him. "We could make a cave, a bit like the thought-wolves made in the tree roots."

"There aren't exactly any trees here, Arty," Maudie said.

"No, he's right, it's a great idea. We dig a snow cave and wait out the storm. We need a snow ridge – it'll make it easier," said Harriet.

"There," said Maudie, pointing westwards.

As the sky darkened further, they trudged over

to the ridge and began digging an entrance hole. Maudie and Felicity scooped out a cavity, while Arthur and Harriet cleared the snow they had dug to stop it blocking the entrance. They didn't say a word, and Arthur's jaw felt so frozen tight he couldn't speak if he'd wanted to.

Soon it was completely dark. They were buffeted by a wind that almost knocked them from their feet. Harriet clipped her safety rope to Arthur and even though it felt impossible, the temperature dropped further. The snow swirled around them so they couldn't see anything apart from their dark shapes in a spiral of white.

Still they dug, with quivering breaths, as the icy temperatures bit all around.

When it seemed as bad as it could get, the ferocity of the storm grew more intense. The freezing wind hit, howling with anger and shooting shards of ice. Arthur felt sure in another few seconds they would become statues. He shook uncontrollably, and he couldn't feel his body any more.

"One last push," Harriet stuttered as they dug a few more scoops. Then she hurried Arthur into the hole and followed.

"We need to build up the door to protect ourselves," said Maudie.

They all scooped more from the walls around them to build the door. They fought to keep it in place, while the wind and snow hurled and whistled outside.

Soon the gap was filled and the raging snowstorm grew muffled. They sat with their legs tucked in, squished together, teeth chattering and bodies shaking. After a moment, Harriet reshaped an area of the wall into a shelf and placed a candle on it. "If that goes out, we'll need an opening and air quickly. You try to sleep, and I'll keep watch."

"We'll take turns," said Felicity through blue lips.

"I'll go first," said Arthur.

"Then me," said Maudie.

Harriet smiled. "All right. A chime each."

All they could do was keep as close together as possible and try to sleep while listening to the fierce growl of the wind and the battering outside.

And wait.

After Arthur's watch, he woke Maudie. "Hey, it's your turn."

She rubbed her eyes and nodded. As he closed his eyes she whispered, "I was dreaming of Dad, back on the *Violetta*. There's something that I can't shake, Arty."

He opened his eyes. "What is it?"

"We know that Eudora Vane did this, but it's so calculated; all planned out. And that story they made up about the fuel theft. She didn't just want to stop them, she wanted to discredit Dad."

He nodded. "I've been thinking the same. We know how she did it, but do we really know why? It feels like there has to be more to it."

Arthur's brain rolled over and over. Eventually, he snuggled his head into Felicity's shoulder and let sleep take him.

*

The absence of noise woke Arthur. The storm had left. There was a small gap in the snow cave above.

Harriet poked her head in, her face big and beaming. "The storm has passed. Are you all right?"

He nodded. He could just about feel his fingers and toes.

"And the others?"

"Still sleeping." His shoulders ached where he'd been scrunched up for so long.

"Will you be able to squeeze through and help me?" she asked.

Even though the last thing he wanted was to leave the meagre warmth that had built up in the snow cave, he nodded and managed to crawl through the opening.

Once outside, the sky was cloudless, as though nothing had happened, and the sun so bright he had to cover his eyes for a moment until he got used to it. He saw Harriet had dug a hole and was making a fire.

"Felicity took two watches; she didn't wake me. But I must admit I slept like a baby!"

Arthur was drawn by her great energy. She was so assured in everything she did. Little had phased her, apart from being penned in the caves. He hoped one day he would be like her.

Together they dug a bigger hole out for the others and set some snow over the heat to melt into water for cooking and drinking. The others soon woke.

Felicity stretched her arms. "I feel as though I've been shaken up by nature's great hand itself and thrown into a heap of frozen bones which have gone back all wrong." She cooked porridge flavoured with dried berries she had gathered in the forest, while the others warmed by the fire.

Maudie insisted on polishing Arthur's iron arm. "You must look your best for the Polaris," she said.

Then they ate, and even though it was a tiny ration, it took away some of Arthur's hunger and warmed him from the inside.

Harriet checked their direction, and they packed quickly. "Well, here we are: the last stage. I think things are going to be a lot easier today," she said with a smile.

They started walking, but Felicity paused.

"What is it?" Arthur asked.

"I've a strange tingling in my toes and I don't like it."

"Keep moving, you need to get your circulation going."

"They're not cold. It's that feeling I get."

They'd only been walking for a few moments more when an enormous boom thrummed through the mountainside behind, stopping them dead.

"What was that?"

They looked behind as another boom punched through the air.

"What's going on?"

"It's stating the obvious, but I think something exploded," said Felicity.

Another huge crash sounded, and snow and rock shot into the air in the distant mountains behind. The explosions kept coming. Parthena took flight and soared away screeching.

"Where are you going? Come back!" Arthur called.

"The noise is likely scaring her," said Felicity.

His calling whistle was lost on the wind. He watched helpless as she flew north-east.

Then everything fell quiet again.

Harriet was glued to the uniscope. "I don't believe it."

She passed the uniscope to Arthur. The crammed mountains now had a narrow slice of sky between them lower down. He swallowed hard. "How far to the Polaris, Harriet?"

"Half a day," she said faintly.

"No wonder they weren't hurrying to chase us under the mountain. She's making her own path straight through; it must've been her plan all along", said Maudie. "That's why we caught up with her more quickly than we expected: it wasn't just the pitch she was carrying, it was a huge amount of explosives."

"But the gap's not big enough to get the *Victorious* through yet," said Arthur.

They stared as another explosion echoed across the land.

Felicity took her lucky spoon from her fur coat and jabbed it angrily in the air. "It's an abomination, doing that to a giant of nature! Who does she think she is?"

"Someone who thinks she can do whatever she wants and get away with it," Harriet said.

Arthur whistled once more for Parthena, but she'd flown from sight.

"She's probably just finding a safe place to hide. That bird has traversed continents; she'll be back," Maudie said.

Arthur took a deep breath and nodded. "We have to go – right now. There's no way we're going to let Eudora Vane get to South Polaris before us, Harriet," he said.

"That's one heck of a look of determination you've got in your eye, Brightstorm." Harriet smiled at him. "And please, call me Harrie. I tell everyone to call me Harriet rather than Captain, but my dearest, closest friends call me Harrie."

A warm glow filled him inside.

"We'll make it first, even if we have to run the whole way." Maudie took Arthur's hand and gave a defiant nod. Then she reached for Harriet's hand and Felicity grasped Arthur's iron fingers. They stood for a moment then let go and trudged onwards.

Arthur no longer felt the vicious bite of the frozen South. The burning need inside of him to make it to South Polaris drove him forward. They maintained a fast and steady trek through the deep snow, with Arthur calling out the rhythm if they slowed.

After two chimes, they paused for Harriet to check co-ordinates with her way-finder. The explosions had stopped and a new sound buzzed in the distance.

The *Victorious* was gaining on them. Arthur could no longer feel his toes or the fingers of his left hand. The relentless pace was taking its toll. But they had to carry on. There was no choice; they had to get justice for Dad. His entire crew had died because of Eudora, and they couldn't let her go down in history for succeeding. They were so close now – one last push.

It was then the great shadow of the *Victorious* loomed behind them.

As the darkness overtook him, Arthur ran, not knowing where the strength came from, his muscles burning, and his ears throbbing with the engine noise. He increased his speed, but the *Victorious* edged in front and he was chasing its shadow; like water through his fingers, it was slipping away. He pushed harder, his lungs on fire, but the ship was too far ahead. His boot caught in the snow. He tripped and rolled, then watched, utterly helpless, as the *Victorious* hovered and lowered, landing directly on the flat indent of South Polaris a short distance ahead.

He sank his face into the snow. The feeling of failure gouged at him. He'd never felt so helpless.

The others were soon with him. They sat in the snow, their shoulders sagged, faces sullen and disbelieving.

No one spoke for a long time.

Anger churned inside Arthur. He fought every urge in his body telling him to run onwards to Eudora and confront her, to find out why she had killed his father's crew. But Arthur knew his rash decisions had cost him before; it had cost Tuyok more. For once he had to stop himself. He pounded the snow with his fist.

Then the crumple of hurried footsteps in snow sounded beside him. It took him a moment to realize what was happening.

Maudie was hurtling towards the *Victorious*.

CHAPTER 28

SOUTH POLARIS

Arthur rushed after her. "Maud, stop!" But she was too fast. He could hear Harriet and Felicity not far behind. The figures of the *Victorious* crew were growing closer with every moment. Eudora posed for a photograph, holding up her instruments and a time-piece as proof.

Maudie was almost there.

"Stop!" he shouted, but it was too late. They'd seen them.

Maudie was shouting. Eudora's crew quickly surrounded her.

"Get your hands off her!" Arthur called.

"Why?" Maudie shouted at the captain of the *Victorious*, while struggling in the grip of two crew members.

A cruel smile spread across Eudora's face. "Well, if it isn't the little orphans. You quite surprise me, again and again. You've somehow managed to scurry through the mountains. Well, I'm sure Daddy would be so proud of you and your upstart natures. And here comes Miss Culpepper. You're a credit to your family name, but I'm afraid you still haven't beaten the Vanes."

"Don't hurt them!" Harriet called, running into the group to stand beside them, closely followed by Felicity.

Smethwyck stepped beside Eudora, his gun pointed at them.

Eudora thought for a moment. "Search them."

Her crew emptied their bags. Arthur's explorer's journal fell in the snow, Harriet's camera, the remains of the poisoned cake, and Dad's diary.

"Why did you do it? It wasn't just about the challenge, was it?" Arthur said.

"Your instincts serve you well. It was never only about getting to South Polaris first. Although the prize *is* the destiny of the Vane legacy and not one I'm prepared to lose." She rooted through the contents of their bags scattered on the ground, making a pile of their evidence, then said, "Burn it."

They watched helplessly as it was destroyed.

"But you still have something that belongs to me." She held out her pink gloved hand.

Arthur frowned. "The locket? It belongs to our Mum and Dad. You stole it from Dad."

Eudora took a step closer. With a soft tilt of her head, she said, "So, little crime solver, let me pose a new mystery – how could I steal a locket from Ernest Brightstorm if an avalanche and an uncrossable broken lake was between us?"

The words weighed like a rock inside of him.

Eudora looked to the sky and laughed, shrill as the biting air around them. "Why, you didn't even think to open it and look inside."

Arthur's trembling hand took the lockets from his neck. Maudie wriggled from the crew member holding her and held out her hand. Arthur placed them in her palm. She helped him click open the first. There was the picture of their parents. They opened the next – inside was a photograph of two little girls.

"Who are they?" Maudie said.

Arthur saw the resemblance instantly. The girl on the left was the younger version of the woman beside Dad in the other locket – the broad smile and dimples below her cheekbones, the slant of her eyes the same as Maudie's. It was Mum. Every muscle in his body tightened – the other girl with elaborately plaited hair and a confident close-lipped smile looked adoringly at the older girl. It was undoubtedly a young Eudora Vane. He put his finger to the picture of his parents in the other locket and pulled. Sure enough, hidden behind was the same picture of the two little girls.

The bottom fell out of his world. "The initials VE – they are for Violetta and Eudora. The lockets belonged to you – you were sisters," he said.

"Your father was no one. Violetta was a Vane – I couldn't believe it when she said she was marrying an outsider nobody, a wannabe explorer without an ounce of true explorer blood in his family. She degraded herself, she dishonoured our name, but she was so under his spell she wouldn't listen to sense. Violetta had such a bright future, then she met your father, and all she cared about was building their sky-ship together. Your father brainwashed her, turned her against me. It wasn't long before she completely disowned our family, saying our greatest achievements were a source of shame to her. Imagine! Disowning the Vane legacy! Well, she got her due: you two disgusting *Brightstorm* brats came along, killing her at your birth."

"Don't you listen to a word from that repulsive mouth of hers," Felicity said, pulling them both close. "Your mother's death was an accident. Bad things happen, but it isn't your fault."

Eudora glanced at Arthur's iron arm. "One look at you and it was proof she was punished for her choices."

"Don't you dare speak about my brother like that."

"A half-formed boy, a constant broken reminder of their mistake."

Maudie lunged for Eudora but the rest of Eudora's crew were poised. Harriet grabbed her back and held her firm – Smethwyck's gun was on her.

"Arthur is already a hundred times the person you'll ever be. They both are," Harriet said.

"Ernest Brightstorm had to pay for taking my sister from me. But I played the long game, and I hid my animosity towards him, made him think he was being accepted by the explorer families of old. And when the first South Polaris challenge came along, I knew it was my chance. In the quiet south, away from all eyes, no one would question a disaster. I had an opportunity to bring down his upstart family name once and for all."

"They loved each other and you will never kill that fact, Eudora," said Harriet.

Eudora straightened her body and lifted her chin. "Love? Love is loyalty, love is knowing where you are from and your duty to legacy, love is family name. The Brightstorm twins have a broken family name which meant nothing before and means even less now."

"You're wrong. Love isn't about bloodlines. Love is what you decide to do – the choices you make," said Arthur.

Felicity waved her lucky spoon at Eudora. "You're wrong about family. You might have taken their father from them, but he's still living on, right inside of them, stronger than ever and fighting back against the terrible injustice put on them. They have family – they have me and Harrie and every other member of our crew waiting back in the forest. Family isn't always what you're born into. It's what you do for each other and the experiences you go through together that makes a family."

"How very touching," Eudora said in a bored tone. "But I'm afraid I have to get going now. Your disappearance will be just as easy – I shall enjoy making up the story. I must admit it gives me quite the thrill seeing all their gullible faces. Although, it seems such a waste of true explorer blood with you, Harriet. However, you are clearly more ambitious than your years, and Lontown will shake their heads at your naive attempt on South Polaris with an untested, higgledy-piggledy ship, and marvel at the Vane crew's attempts to save you on our return journey – such a shame we were too late."

"You're deranged," Arthur said.

"Who first? I'd leave you to freeze, but I think a little insurance is needed. The rest of your crew will perish; that is, after we stop to retrieve some of your water technology, Miss Culpepper. You should consider yourselves lucky! It'll be over before you know it, whereas your crew will suffer long, painful, cold deaths."

Smethwyck pulled back the trigger. "Oldest to youngest," he said, then pointed the gun at Felicity.

She swallowed hard. "I'm not afraid of you and I'm not afraid of dying. But you don't need to harm these two – they're your niece and nephew. Like it or not, they're your blood too."

Arthur had to think quickly. Time hung, just as the sun poised in the sky at the same point in the Polaris, the light flickering, crisp and bright. That's when he knew what to do, but he needed Maudie's help. But how could he let her know?

"Wait!" he said.

Eudora narrowed her gaze. She raised a hand a little, enough to pause Smethwyck.

"I need you to answer one thing for me first."

"Go on."

"Maudie and I need to know something before you shoot us. Only you can tell us." Arthur knew he'd got her attention and had bought the valuable time he needed.

"I'll indulge you. What do you need to know?"

He glanced at Maudie. "What do moths do?"

Maudie looked puzzled.

Eudora's brow creased. She let out an ugly laugh. "What a silly question!"

The bright sun blinked off his iron arm. "Tell us, what do moths do?" he repeated.

Smethwyck stood in front of them, gun wavering, a confused expression. Some other members of the crew laughed.

Arthur saw a smile edging in the corner of Maudie's mouth, and he knew she'd realized.

"They seek the light," she said. Swiftly, she grasped his iron hand and raised it.

The glare of the sun was fierce and bounced off his iron arm, reflecting a stream of light from the flat metal panel with the moth back towards Smethwyck. Quick as a blink, Maudie adjusted the angle so that sunlight flashed straight at Smethwyck's eyes.

"Shoot!" Eudora shouted.

The gun fired.

Arthur's body jolted back as it hit, and he fell backwards. He looked down – there was a scorch mark where the bullet had ricocheted off his iron arm, missing him by a whisker.

A member of the crew cried out as Maudie kicked them away, then more shouts and scuffles as another of the Vane crew wrestled with Felicity. Harriet tussled with Smethwyck and knocked the gun out of his hand. It landed in the snow a distance away. Eudora was nearest and she ran towards it.

"Quick, behind that snow ridge – it's our only chance!" Harriet shouted. "Grab whatever you can!"

Felicity and Maudie pulled Arthur up and the four ran for their lives. Shots fired behind them but Eudora wasn't as sharp with a gun as her tongue, and missed.

They ran up the sides of the bank, adrenaline the only thing making it possible, and rolled over the top and behind the snow ridge before collapsing, panting for breath.

They heard Eudora calling her crew back to the ship.

"She'll take off and shoot us from above!" Harriet cried.

"What do we do? We've got nothing!" said Felicity.

"Arty, are you all right? We need to think of something!"

But Arthur couldn't hear properly. His brain buzzed and his thoughts jumbled.

"He's in shock," said Felicity.

"We need a plan and quick." Harriet looked around and pointed to another ridge. "Come on."

They ran again, but the rumble of engines vibrated the snow as the *Victorious* rose. Soon it would be above them and they'd be exposed.

Arthur looked around, the noise in his head was intense. He suddenly realized it wasn't from the gunshot. There were concerned thoughts bombarding him. "*Where, where?*" they were saying.

It was the thought-wolves.

Parthena's call pierced the cold air as she flew from behind a ridge followed by three thought-wolves, their feet thundering through the snow. Then a fourth appeared – a great white beast. Arthur shook his head, certain he was dreaming, or hearing the thoughts of a ghost. There was no doubt in his mind – the huge white wolf heading straight for him was Tuyok.

"*Tuyok?*" Arthur barely dared to think.

"*Cub,*" Tuyok replied.

"*I'm so glad you're alive.*"

"I'm glad you are too!"

An explosion sounded and snow erupted a short distance away.

"Cannons!" Harriet shouted.

"We must go."

Climbing on to Tuyok's back was like coming home. In an instant, the thought-wolves were charging faster than any living creature he'd ever seen, back towards the mountains. Arthur looked over his shoulder at the *Victorious*, but it was no match for the thought-wolves. With every second, they were getting further away from the black smear of pitch trailing across the perfect sky.

CHAPTER 29

GOODBYE, DAD

Under the shelter of the mountains, they waited until they were certain the *Victorious* was long gone back through the gap it had made in the mountainside. Then they all rested, every one of them physically and emotionally exhausted to the core.

Arthur snuggled into Tuyok's fur. *"But we heard you get shot back near the lake on the* Victorious – *there was silence?"*

"I leapt from the ship and was still in snow for a long time. When I heard their thoughts and what they would do to you, I couldn't let the dark take me

yet. I made it to the forest and my pack found me and took the bullet from my flesh and healed my wound. Then Slartok returned with the others and we heard the death sky-ship destroying the mountain to make their path. The hawk Parthena led the way and we followed to find you."

"Thank you, Tuyok."

Exhausted, the four travellers lay in the warm fur of the thought-wolves. Parthena was beside Arthur. He stroked her head. "So, you flew to find the thought-wolves and lead them to us. You are a brilliant bird. Dad would be proud," he whispered.

Arthur looked over at Maudie and the others, their bodies soon rising and falling with every slow, sleeping breath. As he closed his eyes, Arthur tried to forget Eudora's triumph earlier. We made it out alive, he reminded himself, and that was no doubt a greater victory.

Later, Felicity made sweet tea, which was like nectar and revived them with every sip, washing the fatigue and awfulness little by little from their bodies and minds. Even the thought-wolves tried some and agreed there was an almost magical quality to this strange drink from afar.

It felt good not to be racing any more. Although the stab of failure and losing the evidence was a feeling Arthur knew he would never lose, the truth was now inside him, and it went some way to filling the hole. He felt a great weight had lifted from his shoulders.

When they felt ready to embark on the journey back, Arthur and Maudie visited the ice cave where their father lay. The tunnel had partially collapsed due to vibrations from the explosions, but they were as close as they could get.

Harriet and Felicity left them there alone for a moment to say goodbye, while they readied themselves for the journey over the mountain.

"Dad, we didn't understand what you were trying to tell us by sending Parthena with the locket, but we know now," said Arthur. "We came, for you, and we made it all the way to South Polaris."

"It wasn't quite as we'd hoped it would be, I'm afraid," Maudie said.

"There won't be any reward and we'll have to find a way to make our own way in Lontown. . ."

"But we know we can do it. . ."

Arthur looked sideways at Maudie and smiled.

"Because we did what we came to do – we found the truth."

"And we did lots of cool stuff on the way..."

"We crossed the Second Continent and..."

"We met kings, and we even crossed..."

"The biggest ocean on the planet..."

"Only to survive..."

"Sabotage."

"We'll let you guess who was behind that."

"And we crashed, over the Everlasting Forest..."

"But every crew member lived."

"We met the thought-wolves..."

"And found out how to be friends with them."

"They saved us!"

"Parthena was amazing."

"And all the way, Harrie and Felicity..."

They both fell silent for a moment.

"They've been beside us every step," Maudie began.

"I mean they've really been there for us..."

"Like . . . family."

The twins looked at each other and smiled.

"We're going to be fine, Dad," said Maudie. "And we're going to make you proud, even if we have no evidence left to prove what Eudora Vane did, we're going to rebuild the Brightstorm name. Somehow."

They stood up to leave, but as they did, their torch-flame light caught a curious shape, too square to be a rock. Arthur went over to it. "Maud, it's Dad's camera!"

"Hey, what if it's still working? We could take another picture of the *Violetta*'s fuel stores and at least prove Dad didn't steal from the *Victorious*!"

"Come on, let's tell Harrie."

They both paused.

"I don't want to leave him," Maudie said.

"Then let's leave something here with him, so we're always here," Arthur said.

Maudie took her ribbon from her hair. Then Arthur remembered the page from *Volcanic Islands of the North*. It had been in his arm all this time. He could get another copy back in Lontown.

He unfolded the paper and read. "The Brightstorm moth, a new species discovered by Ernest Brightstorm in the Northern Isles, uses the light of the moon to ensure they travel in an absolutely straight line, allowing them to navigate successfully between two volcanic islands fifty miles apart, and never stray from their path."

Together they tied it around a rock using Maudie's ribbon – their two hands working as one.

*

They found the thought-wolves with Harriet and Felicity on the mountainside ready to depart. The aurora rippled faintly across the great beautiful plain of South Polaris, dancing in its glorious colours.

"There's a sight I'll never forget," Felicity said with a sigh.

"I could murder that woman for destroying my camera," Harriet huffed.

Arthur smiled and held out his father's camera. "We found it in the tunnel close to him – is there a chance it'll still work?"

Harriet examined it. "There's still film in there. It's a bit battered, but it's worth a try."

"Maudie and I thought we could retake the photographic evidence from the *Violetta* on the way back, to show the fuel supplies were empty."

"That's a brilliant idea." Harriet smiled. "But first I think we should capture this moment." Then she carefully arranged the camera on a rock and Maudie helped her set an automatic timer. They posed for a picture with the thought-wolves, with the great plain and southern aurora behind.

"Well, there's a picture we may at least be able to make good money with in Lontown, and perhaps we can get a few more of the mountains on the way back, to sell to the Geographical Society," said Harriet.

"It'll certainly be a memory picture, that's for sure." Felicity sat on a rock and looked around one last time. "I must say, this is the first time my feet have felt rested in over a moon-cycle."

They all laughed.

"Ready?" Harriet said.

They nodded and climbed on their thought-wolves. Arthur felt comforted; Tuyok's fur was as soft and warm as Dad's arms around him.

*

After two days travelling through the scarred mountainside, they carefully made the treacherous journey back over the frozen lake, then to the *Violetta* where they retook the pictures of the empty fuel stores, and finally back into the forest. In another two days, the small clearing where the *Aurora* had crashed came into view. But there was no sign of the crew, only a few odd scraps of the ship.

"Where in all of the Wide have they vanished to?" Felicity said.

"You don't think…" Arthur's heart sank in his chest as he had the awful thought that something terrible had happened to them at Eudora's hands.

Harriet looked across at him. "Welby will have put steps in place to protect everyone, I'm certain."

Tuyok sniffed the air. "*To the west.*"

"He knows where they've gone!" Arthur said.

The thought-wolves took them a little further west, following the scent trail. After a while the thought-wolves stopped in a small darkened clearing. There was a rustling of leaves, and figures cautiously emerged from behind the trees.

"Welby, is that you?" Harriet called. "Don't be afraid of the wolves. They're very friendly, and ever so remarkable!"

With some trepidation, the crew came forward, but it wasn't long before they embraced their friends warmly.

The relief at seeing Harriet was clear on Welby's

usually unreadable face. "Your parents would not have forgiven me if you'd not come back," he said to her seriously.

Harriet gave him a firm pat on the arm. "It'll take more than the Third Continent and that woman to stop us. A wise decision to move, Welby."

"Naturally we suspected she may return at some point, so we created a concealed camp. We heard her pass by not two days ago."

Queenie purred excitedly to see Harriet, and brushed happily around her legs, then went straight to Maudie and with a "Prwwwt mwwwt," jumped into her arms.

"She's glad we're all right," Maudie said.

The crew had made a great canopy above the clearing, disguising the rebuild of the sky-ship. It looked unrecognizable. The crew had worked diligently under Welby's capable command and had made half of the *Aurora* into what looked like a workable ship.

"We've bypassed the secondary hydra-pump and rewired the hydro-converter," Welby declared.

"That was a genius idea, Welby," Maudie said, impressed.

"I'm not your average butler," he said with a wink. "She's half a sky-ship but a fair good half, which should get us back to the Second Continent with a bit more work. I can't quite find the best way to connect the two with a single valve. I've been waiting for you to help me, if you could lend me your expertise, Miss Brightstorm?"

"I knew you needed us, Welby. We're not just children, eh?" She smiled and got to work.

*

The ship was almost ready. With a few tweaks, and by melting enough snow for the engine, they were ready to set sail the next day. It was time to say a sad farewell to the thought-wolves. Arthur squeezed his arm tightly around Tuyok's neck and found he couldn't speak, so he simply thought, "*Friend.*"

"*Friend,*" said Tuyok.

After a long time holding on, Arthur eventually said. "*Maybe one day I'll come back to visit, in my own sky-ship.*"

"*You are welcome in our pack any time,*" said Tuyok. The thought-wolves dipped their heads, then turned and sped into the trees, disappearing into the gloom. As the half-ship *Aurora* took off, their farewell howls sounded across the forest.

The weather was kind to the crew, and after half a moon-cycle they were back in the Second Continent Citadel. Batzorig and Temur patched up the *Aurora,* insisting they wouldn't take a sovereign for supplies or labour and filling their ship with wonderful foods. After several more weeks they reached the Culldam Sea and were soon flying over the First Continent's green fields.

It was mid-morning break. Harriet steadied the wheel while everyone else lounged on deck eating spiced egg-free buns, which Felicity had named home buns to celebrate their return.

Arthur leant over the side of the ship, viewing the farms below through the uniscope: farmers sowing seeds and cows lazing in the fields. "It's funny: it's as though nothing has changed down there, yet everything has changed up here."

"I know what you mean," said Maudie.

Although he wasn't entirely sure she did. He could still see the Maudie-shaped hole there in Lontown waiting to be filled in the future at

Lontown Universitas. But for him, it felt like the end, not the start.

"Are you all right?" Maudie said.

He nodded. "Never better."

Maudie put her arms around him and hugged him tight. He wrapped his arm as far around her as he could.

"You have more hug in one arm than Eudora has in her little finger," Maudie said.

"But I still can't believe we're half Vane." Arthur stuck out his tongue and pulled a face.

"Yes, I vote we don't mention it again. I don't think Auntie Eudora has the best ring to it."

They laughed.

Felicity came over, taking a couple of marsh cakes from her pocket and passed them one each.

Harriet handed over the watch of the wheel to Welby and joined them. "So, you never did tell me how your need for a remarkable iron arm came about in the first place?"

"The truth is, even though Maudie's stories are far more exciting, I was just born like this."

Harriet smiled. "You know, you've got a real talent for problem-solving and seeking out the truth, and they're important skills for any explorer."

It felt good to hear her say that.

"I thought we'd lost our future when we lost Dad. Because we were going to do these things together, the three of us, as a family."

"Control is an illusion. We never know what life will throw at us. You are the master of your destiny, Arthur, and you can still do those things. Your father is still with you, inside." Harriet smiled and lingered as though she was contemplating something. "I wanted to ask you both a question," she said eventually.

They looked at her curiously.

"I know I failed us all by not winning the sovereigns, but I have some savings which will be paid to the crew and yourselves. It's not a patch on what we could have had, but it will compensate everyone fairly for what they have put in. And I wondered, that is, if you would like to, if you would come and live at Number Four Archangel Street when we get back? The house will only be half the size it used to be, at least for a while, mind you! But there will be no need for you to go back to that vile place in the Slumps, and if the

Begginses have anything to say about it, I'll soon set them right. Felicity has agreed to stay on as cook. Welby can be a bit grumpy, but he's all right, really, and I can't promise I'm the easiest to live with on account that I can't sit still for more than a few minutes, but. . ."

"Yes!" they both jumped in. "We'd like it more than anything."

CHAPTER 30

VICTORIOUS

The day they arrived back in Lontown and set down at Number Four Archangel Street, the crowds built quickly. The crew spent some time securing the *Aurora* in place, as many of the mechanisms that had transformed the *Aurora* had been destroyed in the crash, so she looked more like a ship nestled between houses than a house. Harriet explained to the questioning crowd that they were tired from their journey, and would make a statement about their expedition in the following days. The crew busied about manually adjusting great panels, cogs whirring and clunking until an almost house-like shape was restored. Then the twins said a sad goodbye to the rest of the crew, who returned to their families in Lontown, and Harriet closed the shutters to the people outside.

Later, when Harriet, Felicity, Maudie and Arthur were in the galley having tea, Welby brought in some copies of the *Lontown Chronicle* that had been issued that morning. *Eudora Vane – Victorious!* the headline glowed. Her perfect smile beamed from the page.

Arthur read on:

> Eudora Vane returned after successfully completing the challenge to be the first human to reach South Polaris. The rival explorers, led by young Harriet Culpepper, are believed to have perished as their ship crashed in the Third Continent. The *Victorious* saw the remains of a crash, and many paw prints, so it is assumed that the crew has sadly met the same fate as the *Violetta*'s. The winnings will be awarded at a special ceremony at the Geographical Society this evening at the chime of eight.

He threw the paper down. "It makes me sick to think she's got away with it."

"Well, they'll soon have to retract the report on the fate of the *Aurora*, seeing as we're back safely, not a crew-member lost," said Maudie proudly. "Eudora must have heard about our return by now; I wonder what she's thinking!"

"Probably trying to come up with a way to discredit us," said Harriet.

"I still think we should tell the police – the Geographical Society – somebody!" Arthur cried, angrily kicking at a footstool.

Harriet frowned and shook her head. "I know how you feel, Arthur, believe me, I do. But we need evidence in order to make accusations like that. Eudora is very powerful, so calling her a murderer without proof would only backfire. She's dangerous – that much is abundantly clear. And I don't think there's any way to prevent her from claiming the prize. It's far from ideal, but we may at least be able to sell the photographs we took with your father's camera."

"And show the one of the *Violetta* fuel reserves to the Geographical Society and at least clear his name of breaking the code." Arthur took the camera from his bag and passed it to Harriet.

*

Later that day, Arthur dozed in his bunk, listening to the noises of Lontown – chattering voices in the street, the distant rumble of sky-ships and the frequent chimes of the watchtowers. Part of him was pleased to be back, but part craved the absolute silence of the far south.

Harriet and Maudie burst into the room. They both grinned widely.

"What the clinking cogs has got into you two?" he said sitting up.

Maudie pulled him out of bed. "You need to see this."

Photographs were spread on the galley table.

"I developed the film. There were some that your Dad took. This was the last one."

There was Ernest Brightstorm – looking pale and thin, but holding up his way-finder and timepiece, the sun and moon behind him.

"Does that say ninety degrees south?" Arthur said. He couldn't believe what he was seeing. The picture in front of them was Ernest Brightstorm at South Polaris – just over a year ago.

"When we found him, we assumed he'd died on his way, because his diary stopped when he'd run out of pencil – we didn't even consider he could have been on his way back," Maudie said.

Arthur could barely breathe. "He made it – he was the first person ever to reach South Polaris!"

The chimes of the *Lontown Chronicle* Tower began striking eight.

He looked at Harriet with panic. "How far is the Geographical Society?"

"It's not far, but we'll have to run."

In moments, they were dashing through the streets towards the great domed building. They pushed past security, with Felicity waving her spoon threateningly at the guards. Harriet led the way through the grand hallways until they faced the huge double doors. Arthur and Maudie pushed one each and burst into the auditorium.

"Stop!" Arthur yelled, holding the picture high.

Eudora Vane stood on the dais with the well-dressed board of the Geographical Society. The bank draft for one million sovereigns wavered between Madame Gainsford's hand and Eudora's.

"What is the meaning of this intrusion?" Madame Gainsford said. The furry stoat around her neck raised its head and stared.

The four of them hurried through the audience to the stage.

"This is quite irregular," one of the board said.

"Barging in like vagrants from the Slumps," said another.

Eudora looked as though she had seen a ghost, but then her perfect veneer returned. She put her hand to her heart. "Harriet Culpepper and the Brightstorm children made it home against all odds. Well, how extraordinary – simply wonderful. Perhaps you should show them to the back chambers. They must be quite fatigued!"

"We're fine," Arthur said stiffly, stomping on to the stage. "This photograph proves Ernest Brightstorm was the first person to make it to South Polaris."

The audience gasped.

Eudora's cheeks turned a shade of pink which matched her outfit perfectly.

"Do you need to sit down, Madame Vane? This must be such a shock to you," Maudie said dryly.

Madame Gainsford took the picture. "This certainly looks like Ernest Brightstorm – naturally it will need thorough investigation, but I declare until such a time the winnings must remain in the care of the Society."

Eudora nodded. "Of course."

Arthur stared open-mouthed. It wasn't quite the reaction he'd expected. He'd imagined Eudora furious, screaming, indignantly protesting, but certainly not this.

"We will need to speak to you, of course, Miss Culpepper, and the Brightstorm twins, but this does appear to have turned these proceedings on their head somewhat."

Eudora smiled sweetly. "I will retire and await news."

The four of them watched her leave the auditorium. Felicity hugged Harriet, and Maudie hugged Arthur.

The Geographical Society board said they would be in touch soon. Outside Harriet and Felicity walked in front chatting happily and Arthur and Maudie lingered behind, feeling content but confused at Eudora's submissive reaction.

As they passed through an alley, a figure suddenly appeared, blocking their path.

It was Smethwyck. The twins turned to retreat, only to find Eudora standing behind them, smiling sweetly.

"Hello, children," she said.

Arthur glanced at Maudie, trying to catch her eye. Should they scream? Try to fight?

Eudora slowly turned up her sleeve to show her explorer tattoo. "There are traits of explorer families which cannot be denied. They run thick through your veins; such things are not an option. Maybe I was wrong about you. Perhaps there's more of the Vane family in you than I could have ever considered." She looked them up and down.

"We're nothing like you," Maudie said.

Eudora smiled. "You're so loyal, Maudie. You could have become a great engineer and been spared this messy business, if not for your brother. But you knew Arthur wouldn't stop until he had the answers, and you had to make sure he stayed alive. You show great potential."

Arthur's stomach clenched – Eudora Vane had a skill for reading deep inside of people. It made him feel vulnerable. She turned to him. Miptera was back in brooch position on Eudora's jacket. She scuttled to Eudora's shoulder and unfurled her wings. One was pinned and slightly crooked from when Tuyok had jumped on her. She clacked her mandibles at him.

"And you, Arthur – such single-minded ambition. You remind me of someone."

Arthur squirmed.

"That you made it back here against all odds is testament to a strong will. I'm almost . . . impressed."

The last thing Arthur wanted was her admiration.

"We made it because we have friends, something you'll never have," Maudie said.

"You seem very composed, considering you've lost," Arthur said.

She shrugged. "The adoration from reaching South Polaris first would have been thrilling, but now the people of Lontown will love me even more, because I came so close and was robbed by a dead man. I'm sure the *Lontown Chronicle* can put quite a spin on it. There are plenty of other conquests in this world to take on, and Lontown will be rooting for me." She reduced her voice to a whisper. "And you forget – I already took my prize."

"Killing our dad and his crew was not a prize!" Arthur said.

Eudora smiled. "I'll be watching you, twins. Perhaps I'll call this a draw in the battle." She leant in. "But I never lose a war."

Although it made him sick to look at her, he matched her stare. "There's always a first time, Aunt."

Then Eudora smiled sweetly, turned, and left.

CHAPTER 31
HOME

Many weeks later in Lontown, the *Aurora* was playing at being a house once again. There was still only one floor, but Maudie was busily drawing up the second tier along with Harriet and Welby.

They were taking a break in the library when Felicity walked in barefooted, carrying a toppling tray of tea and marsh cakes. Everyone else had taken off their shoes, due to Felicity's suggestion of no-shoe Mondays, which she said was nothing short of complete foot liberation. Welby refused, but Maudie and Arthur hid his polished shoes on the roof so he was forced to join in.

Welby rushed into the room waving the *Lontown Chronicle* and passed it to Arthur.

Arthur read the title and his heart soared.

Brightstorm Family Name Cleared

He stood and read on:

> In breaking news, Ernest Brightstorm has been cleared of all accusations, and declared wrongly charged in the case of breaking the Explorer's Code during the ill-fated first Polaris Challenge. The *Lontown Chronicle* and the Geographical Society has therefore agreed the prize money should be divided between the relatives of those who perished on the *Violetta*, and Arthur and Maudie Brightstorm, Ernest's two surviving children. Evidence brought back by the Culpepper expedition has also proved the docile nature of the great fauna of the Third Continent, previously believed to have been vicious beasts. These wolf-like creatures are, it turns out, highly intelligent super sapients. The new theory is that the cause of death of the Brightstorm crew was

> a monumental tragedy: ingestion of a poisonous herb, which the cook mistakenly added to the crew's meal. The poisonous cakes were thought to be avoided by Ernest Brightstorm on account of his egg allergy. With his crew deceased, Ernest Brightstorm went forward alone and succeeded in reaching South Polaris. Knowing he was without hope of rescue before supplies ran out, he bravely carried on and managed to win glory for himself and his crew.

"So, Eudora still gets away with it, but we at least get some of the reward – that'll certainly help with repairs," said Maudie.

"Just her style to contrive that the dead take the blame," Arthur muttered.

"She's got too many allies in the right places. This is the best result we could have hoped for with our lack of other evidence," Harriet said.

"There's no sense looking backwards now." Felicity circled the room topping up everyone's cup of honeyed tea, pausing to fluff Arthur's windswept hair.

He smiled with cheeks stuffed with marsh cake. "And now we have a claim on Brightstorm House, and the rest of Dad's insured property. We can help fund the rest of the *Aurora*'s reconstruction!" Arthur turned the newspaper over. As much as he hated that Eudora had got away with murder, at least she hadn't claimed South Polaris, and he finally knew the truth.

A small article on the back caught his eye:

Ermitage Wrigglesworth Mysteriously
Disappears in the Eastern Isles

"What is it?" Maudie said curiously, looking up from her engineering book. He held the newspaper out to her.

Harriet peered over and read too.

Everyone fell silent. Arthur lifted the cuff of his shirt with his iron fingers and looked at the Brightstorm moth, newly tattooed on his left wrist in fire red and gold. "There's bound to be a trail that leads to the answer," he said.

"It says here that his family will reward richly for his safe return." Maudie retied the new red ribbon in her hair.

Wiggling her toes, Felicity said, "I've always

wanted to get my hands on the eastern moco bean. They say the flavour is the best in the Wide."

"Well, this sounds like a challenge to me. What do you say, Arthur?" There was that undeniable twinkle in Harriet's eye.

Arthur hesitated: Maudie had her studies; she could make it to Universitas within a few years if she worked hard. She looked at him and shook her head. "Arty, you don't seriously think I'd let you have all the fun without me? I can bring my engineering books with me, you know!"

Parthena gave an emphatic screech and Queenie brushed against Arthur's leg and purred. She winked an amber eye at him.

The world was so full of colour and laughter at Number Four Archangel Street, it would be hard to leave Lontown – except of course the *Aurora* would be with them. Arthur looked around at the warm faces gazing back at him. Even Welby had a quiet smile on his lips.

A surge of excitement rose in Arthur's stomach.

Maudie grinned at him. "I know I'm ready for another adventure. What about you, Arthur?"

"Me? I'm a Brightstorm. I was born ready."

ACKNOWLEDGEMENTS

In writing this book I became increasingly aware of how many parallels there are between the writing process and expeditions (there's probably an essay in there somewhere…). I'm lucky enough to have been surrounded by a great crew on this writing journey – one well worthy of the *Aurora*.

To all the team at Scholastic, I can't thank you enough for getting 'on-board' with this story. The Brightstorm twins couldn't have found a better home. Special thanks to my lovely editor, Linas Alsenas – I'm in awe of your keen eye and inspiring mind. I owe endless thanks to you for your enthusiasm, ideas, and for saying yes! Your advice is always so sound and in tune – I've absolutely loved working with you – and it's always time for tea! Also, thanks to designer Jamie for all his brilliant work and to the copyeditors involved for their super observant eyes.

Huge thanks to brilliant illustrator George Ermos, whose fantastic cover art truly blew me away and made me want to jump into the adventure!

Thank you to the marvellous Kate Shaw – the best agent I could ever have hoped for. You set me on a path to true north with your astute story eyes and well-placed words of wisdom. Your belief in me has meant the world. I do believe something of you has seeped into Harriet Culpepper…

I am so fortunate to have made writer friends for life in Jennifer Killick, Lorraine Gregory and James Nicol – you three are not only wondrous writer confidants but very best friends. Thank you wholeheartedly for being jolly fine beta readers and expert fellow mischief-makers. I can't think of three better people to be my first mates.

Imogen Cooper, Vanessa Harbour and all the team of editors and writers at Golden Egg Academy, especially Abigail Kohlhof, Bella Pearson, Anthony Burt, Rus Madon, Kay Vallely, Emma Greenwood, Kirsten Wild and Andrew Wright – you've been a crucial part of my writing journey and your continued friendship and support is like a teacup in a storm – thank you! Also to the community of children's writers and bloggers, you really are the best bunch of humans in the whole Wide. Thank you for being creative, enthusiastic you!

Thank you, Kate Elton, the first writer I met on my journey – you're always there to happy dance with me and I love that we are on this (long!) road together. A special thank you to Mr Dunham, our English teacher. I've no idea where you are, but I would love to think that this may find you somewhere in your retirement, and you will know that you started something magical when you gave us free writing journals. Dave Swann at Chi and Susannah Waters at Sussex, fantastic creative writing lecturers who both inspired me loads – thank you!

To all the rest of my family, friends, and work colleagues who have supported me (far too many to mention, but you know who you are), thank you! Nicola Wilding, thank you for your tips, which helped me think harder about Arthur's world – I can't wait to see your final 'iron arm', and Lucy Denyer O'Leary, your chats and enthusiasm are really appreciated! Thanks, Mum; my niece, Sienna; and sis-in-law Vicky for reading excerpts, bouncing ideas with me and being star cheerleaders. To my core crew Meg, Sammy, Poppy and Darren, thank you for not rolling your eyes at me (too much) when I rambled on about sky-ships, thought-wolves and other bonkers imaginings, and for always believing in me – you're the best. Also sorry for all the weekends I ignored you. PS to my lovely husband who has been waiting to read this until it's a 'real book' – no excuses now!

Oh, and how could I forget ... Bear Grylls – thank you. Your programmes have been my go-to for a few of the situations Arthur stumbles (falls headfirst) into, and should I find myself tripping into quicksand, I like to think I'm rather better equipped now.

Lastly, to you, lovely reader – this world is yours to explore now. A warm welcome to the crew of the *Aurora* – grab your compasses, binoscopes and resilience as you shut the door! It's really good to have you on-board.